POWERS OF THE MIND

The silent voice came into his head like a cold cleansing wind, islanding his consciousness in the eye of the hurricane of noise and fear. It was laden with encouragement to accept what was happening. This wasn't a random concept picked up by himself, but a deliberate projection with the force of years of mental discipline.

Then a helicopter dropped into view, and he found strength in terror.

NO NO NO LEAVE ME ALONE!

The thought blasted out unaimed, and the copter directly above him reacted as if he had riddled it with gunfire. Its nose dipped, it twisted, jerked crazily as one of its outstretched legs crashed into the wall. It fell crunching among piled rubble, and the rotor blades snapped like dry sticks.

Unbelieving, Howson watched it crash, hardly daring to accept that he could be responsible.

Yet he knew he was . . .

Also by John Brunner
published by Ballantine Books:

THE SHEEP LOOK UP

THE SHOCKWAVE RIDER

STAND ON ZANZIBAR

THE SQUARES OF THE CITY

The Whole Man

John Brunner

A Del Rey Book

BALLANTINE BOOKS • NEW YORK

A Del Rey Book
Published by Ballantine Books

Portions of this novel are based on material previously
published in substantially different form in magazines, viz.:

CITY OF THE TIGER, copyright 1958 by Nova Publications,
    Ltd., for *Science Fantasy*, copyright 1959 by Great American
    Publications, Inc. for *Fantastic Universe;*
THE WHOLE MAN, copyright 1959 by Nova Publications,
    Ltd., for *Science Fantasy;*
CURATIVE TELEPATH, copyright 1959 by Great American
    Publications, Inc., for *Fantastic Universe.*

ISBN 0-345-27088-6

Manufactured in the United States of America

First Edition: August 1964
Fourth U. S. Printing: September 1977

First Canadian Printing: October 1964

Cover art by Murray Tinkelman

Spiritus intus alit, totamque infusa per artus
Mens agitat molem et magno se corpore miscet.

Vergil: *Aeneid*, VI, 726-7

Book One   Molem

i

After the birth they put her in a bed, a large woman wasted by worry and hunger, so that it was not only over her emptied belly that her skin hung old-clothes fashion. In spite of her wide pelvic girdle she had had a difficult labor; the tired-faced doctor had judged her a few per cent worse off than those others who competed for space in the hospital ward, so she had been allotted the bed. She showed no sign of appreciation. She would have shown no sign of resentment, either, if she had been treated the same as most other women passed through the delivery room that day, and taken to an armchair to rest for a mere couple of hours while they scrubbed down the floor with a solution of caustic soda, for lack of disinfectant, burned the kraft paper off the delivery table and put on fresh, for lack of laundry facilities.

The "crisis" had been gestating just about as long as the child. It had culminated a week or two ahead of him. There were two panes out from the window next to her bed, and the gaps had been covered with newspaper and adhesive tape. The woman in the bed on the right had a gunshot wound and lay with puzzled eyes staring at the ceiling. In one corner of that ceiling was the trace left by a licking tongue of greasy smoke, exactly the same shade of black-edged-with-gray as would have been left by a candle, but two feet wide.

From the street noise came, unfamiliar, disturbing. Last month there would have been the drone of traffic, a buzz of people wandering in sunlight, a predictable, comforting background with commonplace associations. Now

there was the occasional hoarse shout, grossly amplified, but blurred by the direction of the portable loud-
speaker so that it was impossible to tell more than that
orders were given. Also there was the growl-rumble-
clank of a heavy tracked vehicle; the acid bite of police
whistles; the stamping of unison feet. Automatically the
mind tensed, wondering whether there would follow the
stammer of guns.

An hour or so after the birth a woman in olive-green
battle dress came to the door of the ward. Her hair was
cut man-short and there was a belt with a shiny brown
holster strapped around her waist. She looked about her
curiously and went away.

Another hour, and an old man came pushing a squeaky
trolley with two urns on it, one containing watery soup
and one containing watery coffee. There was also bread.
A nurse hurried in directly after and distributed bowls
and mugs to those patients who could eat.

And a little later still another nurse came, her face
drawn and her mouth downturned, with the doctor who
had supervised the delivery.

Every available bed was in use; only the fact that there
weren't more beds had ensured that floor space was left
between patient and patient. Awkwardly, sometimes having to sidle, the nurse and doctor came to the new mother.

"You . . . uh . . ." The doctor changed his mind about
putting it that way, cleared his throat, tried again. "You
haven't seen your baby yet, Mrs. . . . ?"

"Miss," said the woman in the bed. Her eyelids rolled
down like blinds over her lackluster eyes. Her hair tangled untidily on the pillow, dark and greasy. "Miss Sarah
Howson."

"I see." The doctor wasn't sure if he did or didn't, but
the remark filled a silence even though the silence
was subjective, already occupied in reality by the clang-
ing of empty tin bowls as they were collected after the
patients' meal.

The nurse whispered something to the doctor, showing him a roneotyped form: square gray lines on gray
paper. He nodded.

"I'm sorry about the delay, Miss Howson," he said.
"But things are difficult at the moment. . . . Have you

chosen a name for him yet?" And, catching himself because he was never sure under present circumstances how far the normal routine had actually deteriorated: "You were told you have a boy, weren't you?"

"I guess so. Yes, somebody did say." The woman rolled her heavy head from side to side as though seeking an impossible position of comfort.

"If you've chosen a name, we can enter it on the record of the birth," the doctor prompted.

"I . . . " She rubbed her forehead. "I guess . . Say, are you the doctor who was there?" Her eyes opened again, searched his face. "Yes, you're the one. Doc, it was bad, wasn't it?"

"Yes, it was pretty bad," the doctor agreed.

"Did it . . . ? I mean, is there permanent . . . ?"

"Oh, no, there's no permanent damage," the doctor cut in, hoping to sound reassuring in spite of his splitting headache and gut-souring exhaustion. He wasn't sure of anything any more, it seemed—no one was, currently—but it was a habit to be reassuring.

Where had it all gone? How? The safe calm world of a few weeks back had split apart, and they said "crisis" without explaining anything. To most people it meant nothing of itself; it was just that a bus didn't show at your regular stop, and the electricity failed in the middle of cooking dinner, and there was a slogan of half-finished, smeared letters of red paint, on the sidewalk, and a monument to a dead hero had tilted crazily on its shattered plinth, and the prices of food had soared, and the radio groaned old records and said every fifteen minutes that people should be calm.

Also to the doctor it meant probing hideous wounds for bits of stone and splinters of glass; it meant shortages of disinfectant, antibiotics and even blankets; it meant concussion, shot-wounds and homemade incendiary bombs thrown through the windows.

Now there were the strange uniformed men speaking a dozen languages, standing on street corners with their guns easily slung; there were officers who came asking questions about needed supplies and surplus bed space if any; there were food-ration stands at big intersections and measured handouts of basic nourishment, fol-

lowed by the stamping of the left hand with a one-day
indelible ink to prevent you from coming back until tomorrow—all as though the population had been turned
at a blow into a blend of criminals and charity patients.

"Oh, damn," said the mother, head rolling anew. "I
hoped never to go through that again. And I still could,
huh?"

The nurse gave a sour glance at the doctor, who forced
himself back to the present. The idea was to get the name
fixed in the woman's mind, to displace the simple idea
"baby," to offer some sort of handle to her when she was
compelled to grasp the facts.

"Have you chosen a name for your son?" the doctor
demanded loudly.

"Name? Well . . . Gerald, I gueess. After his father."
Beginning to reveal puzzlement, the woman gazed directly at the doctor and frowned. "What's this all about,
anyway? Why didn't you bring him to me long ago? Is
there something wrong?"

The hell with soft-pedaling. The hell with finesse. The
doctor said shortly, "Yes, I'm sorry to tell you there is."

"Such as what? No arms, no legs?"

"No, nothing so bad, fortunately. There's a . . . a gen-
eralized deformity. It may well be possible to put it right,
in time, of course; it's too soon to say, though."

The woman stared for a long moment. Then she gave
a harsh chuckle.

"Well, God damn! Isn't that just like the bastard? He
wouldn't marry me—said there wasn't anything certain
enough about the world to make plans for life. . . . So
then when I'd been through it—I was telling myself—at
least I'd have a son for my old age—heh-heh—and here's
a cripple I have to support instead of—" The chuckling
returned, and ran together into a dull shuddering moan.

"How about the father?" the doctor said, swallowing
against nausea. Call this a part of the "crisis," too: it
didn't help.

"Him? He was killed. I thought that was how he'd end
up, you know, once it came down to fighting. Oh, God, oh,
God."

"We'll bring you your son now, Miss Howson," the
nurse said.

When the doctor got back to the ward office there was the short-haired woman waiting for him. She had taken off the jacket of her battle dress and hung it on a peg while she went through the records of admission. The national insignia on the shoulder said ISRAEL. The doctor thought irrelevantly that she didn't look like a Jewess with her scalpel-thin nose and piercing blue eyes.

"A woman called Howson," she said, looking up. "We had a dossier on a man named Gerald Pond, whose body was found near the reservoir they dynamited right at the start of the rising. He's supposed to have had a woman friend called Howson."

"That could be right," the doctor said. He dropped limply into a chair. "I just delivered her of a son. Crippled."

"Badly?"

"One shoulder higher than the other, one leg shorter than the other, spinal deformity—pretty much of a mess." The doctor hesitated. "You're not thinking of taking her in for questioning, for heaven's sake! She had a hell of a time on the delivery table, and now she has to face the shock of the kid—it's monstrous!"

"Don't jump to conclusions," said the Israeli woman. "Where is she?"

"In the ward. Fourth bed from the end."

"I'd like to take a look at her."

She rose. The doctor made no move to accompany her. He waited till she was out of the room, then went behind the desk at which she had been sitting and took out from a drawer the last cigarette in the last pack he had. He had lighted it and returned to his chair before she came back.

"Are you arresting her?" he asked sourly.

"No." The Israeli woman sat down briskly and made a note on the carbon copy of a list she was consulting. "No, she's not involved with the terrorists. She's about as apolitical as one can get and still talk coherently. She was afraid of being left alone—she must be what: forty? —and she didn't believe that this man Pond meant exactly what he said. He regarded sex as a necessary act and her as a routine provision. She kidded herself into thinking she could break through his obsession with revolution and sabotage and reduce him to . . . wedding bells, furniture on credit, all that. . . ." She gave a wry smile. "Sad, isn't it?"

"You have a dossier on her, too, presumably," said the doctor in a sarcastic tone. "You didn't get details like that on the spur of the moment."

"Hmmm? No, we have no dossier on her, and it won't be worth the trouble of putting one together, to my mind."

"Oh, marvelous!" the doctor said. "I'm glad to know you draw the line occasionally."

"We don't make the messes, you know," the Israeli woman said. "They just call us in to clear them up."

"Well, hell! If all you have to do is—is walk in that ward and *look* at someone and say there's trouble, yes or no, it's a pity you don't do it before the mess happens instead of afterwards!" The doctor was very tired and, moreover, very resentful of these polyglot strangers with the authority of world opinion at their back; he scarcely knew what he was saying.

He also scarcely knew what the Israeli woman meant when she answered, "There aren't enough of us yet, doctor. Not yet."

ii

After three days they sent Sarah Howson home from the hospital with the child, and also with papers: a nursing mother's emergency ration card, a medical-supply voucher, a medical-inspection voucher, a booklet of formula coupons and a diaper-service voucher.

She came back to the narrow, long street with its double row of identical three-story houses, façades covered in cracked yellow plaster, garbage piled up in the gutters because the "crisis" had stopped municipal collection services. The day after her return, a pair of huge trucks painted the same drab green as the soldiers' uniforms came growling down the street. One ate the garbage with a maw above which a roller brush turned like a dirty mustache; the other hosed the pavement with a smelly germicide. Water was still being sold from carts; it might take months to repair the reservoir Gerald Pond and his companions had so efficiently dynamited, and there was little rain at this time of year.

She spent the first evening back home clearing her two rooms of everything that might remind her of Gerald Pond—old clothes, shoes, letters, books on political subjects. She kept the novels, not to read but because they might be salable. If the baby hadn't been quiet, she would cheerfully have thrown him out with the rest, and Gerald Howson would unknowingly have left the unknowing world.

But he was a passive child, then and always. Hunger might bring a thin crying; the noise didn't last, and he accepted discomfort as a fact of existence, because his distorted body was uncomfortable simply to live in.

The evening little Gerald achieved his first week of individual existence, the soldiers came down the street in an open truck—four of them, and an officer, and a driver. The driver stopped alongside the entrance of the house where Sarah Howson lodged, pulling into a gap between two parked cars but not making any serious attempt to get to the curb. The "crisis" had also interrupted gasoline distribution; the cars here had mostly not moved for a fortnight, and already kids had begun to treat them as abandoned wrecks, slashing the tires, opening the gas-tank caps, scratching names and obscene words on the paint with knives or nails.

The people on the street, the people looking from their cautiously curtained windows, saw the soldiers arrive and felt a stir of nameless alarm. A few of them knew for sure they had done something illegal; a black market had followed the crisis with blurring speed. Many more, adrift on the unfamiliar sea of circumstances, were afraid that they might have infringed some regulation imposed by the pacifying forces, or unwittingly have aided the terrorists. The fact of pacification was scarcely new, but it had been an elsewhere thing: it was reported in the papers and on TV, and it affected people with dark skins in distant countries with jungles and deserts.

Two of the soldiers waited, lounging, by the house door. Their shoulder patches said PAKISTAN and they were tall, good-looking, swarthy, with bright wide smiles, as they exchanged casual comments. But they also carried slung guns.

The other two soldiers and the officer banged on the door until they were admitted. With the frightened landlord they went upstairs, to the top, to Sarah Howson's two rooms. They knocked again there.

When she opened to them, the deflated woman with her big rayon housedress belted to a wide overlap around her waist, the officer was polite, and saluted parade-stiffly. He said, "Miss Sarah Howson?"

"Yes. What is it?" The dark, dull eyes searched the military exterior, seeming to plead for clues to an inward humanity.

"I believe you were formerly an . . . ah . . . an intimate friend of Gerald Pond. Is that correct?"

"Yes." She seemed to sag still more, but there was no protestation in the tone with which she uttered the rest of what she had to say. "But he's dead now. And anyway I never mixed in these political things."

The officer made no comment. He said only, "Well, I must ask you to come with us, please. It is necessary to ask you some questions."

"All right." She stood back apathetically from the door. "Come in and wait while I get changed. Is it going to take long?"

"That depends on you, I'm afraid." The officer shrugged.

"It's the kid, you see." She scuffed at the floor with bare feet. "Do I take him along or try to get someone to mind him for a while?"

The officer frowned and consulted a paper from his pocket. "Oh, that's right," he said after a pause. "Well, you'd better bring him with you, I guess."

They went to police headquarters. There had been blood on the handsome white stone steps, but that was gone now; there were still shrapnel scars and bullet pocks, however, and some smashed windows were still out. The police were no longer in charge. Uniformed or not, they had to show passes on entering, and the armed men guarding the door had shoulder patches saying DENMARK. Sarah Howson looked at them, and not for the first time since Pond's death wondered how he had convinced himself that he and his companions would win out when the world stood ready to act against them.

In the lobby of the building the officer spotted and called to a uniformed woman whose blouse bore white insignia with a red cross instead of the national identification marks. She was pleasant-voiced and smiling, and Sarah Howson let her take the shawl-wrapped bundle of her son.

The smile vanished the instant hands discerned, through the thin cloth, the twisted spine and lopsided shoulders.

"Your baby will be well looked after until you leave," the officer said. "This way, please." He pointed down a door-flanked corridor. "It may be necessary to wait awhile, I'm afraid."

They went to an office overlooking the square in front of the building. The evening sun lighted it, orange and gold over the pale-gray walls and brown and dark-green furniture.

"Sit down, please," the officer said, and went to the desk to pick up the receiver of the intercom. He dialed a three-digit code, and waited.

Then: "Miss Kronstadt, please."

And after a further pause: "Oh, Miss Kronstadt! We have rather an interesting visitor. One of our bright young sanitary experts was down at the municipal incinerators yesterday, getting them back in regular operation, and he happened to spot a name on a letter when it blew out of the truck being unloaded. The name was Gerald Pond. We had him listed for dead, of course, so we didn't follow up until this afternoon, when we found out he had a mistress still living at the same address—"

He stopped, and looked at the phone as though it had bitten him. Rather slowly, he said, "You mean I just send her home? Are you sure she wasn't . . . ? Damn! I'm sorry, I should have checked with you first, but I never thought you'd have reached her so quickly. Okay, I'll have her taken home. . . . What?"

He listened. Sarah Howson felt a stir of interest disperse the cloud of her apathy, and found that if she paid attention she could just catch the words from the phone:

"No, keep her there a few minutes. I'll drop in as soon as I can. I would like to have another chance to see her, though I doubt if we can use more information on Pond then we have already—there's a two-hundred-page dossier here now."

The officer cradled the phone with a shrug and opened the pocket of his jacket to extract a pack of curious cigarettes with paper striped in pale-gray and white. He gave one to Sarah Howson and lighted it for her with a lighter made from an expended shell case.

The door opened and the woman came in briskly—the one with man-short hair and Israeli shoulder patches. Sarah Howson crushed out her cigarette and looked at her.

"I've seen you before," she said.

"That's right." A quick smile. "I'm Ilse Kronstadt. You were in the city hospital when I called there the other day." She perched on the edge of the desk, one leg swinging. "How's the baby?"

Sarah Howson shrugged.

"You're being looked after all right? I mean, you're provided with proper rations, proper services for the kid?"

"I guess so. Not that—" She broke off.

"Not that diaper service and formula coupons help much with the real problem," Ilse Kronstadt murmured. "Isn't that what you were going to say?"

Sarah Howson nodded. Distractedly, she played with the dead butt of her cigarette. Watching her, Ilse Kronstadt began to frown.

"Is it right—about your grandfather, I mean?" she said suddenly.

"What?" Startled, Sarah Howson jerked her head back. "My grandfather—what about him?"

Sympathy had gone from the Israeli woman, as though a light had been turned off behind her eyes. She got to her feet.

"That was *bad,*" she said. "You weren't any shy virgin,

were you? And you knew you shouldn't have children, with your family history! To use a pregnancy as blackmail—especially on a man like Pond, who didn't give a damn about anything except his own dirty little yen for power! *Ach!*" Her accusing gaze raked the older woman like machine-gun fire, and she stamped her foot. The Pakistani officer looked, bewildered, from one to the other of them.

"No, it's not true!" stammered Sarah Howson. "I didn't —I—!"

"Well, it's done now." Ilse Kronstadt sighed, and turned away. "I guess all you can do is try and make it up to the kid. His physical heredity may be all to hell, but his intellectual endowment should be Okay: there's first-rate material on the Pond side, and you're not stupid. Lazy-minded and selfish, but not stupid."

Sullen, resentful color was creeping into Sarah Howson's face. She said after a pause, "All right, tell me: what do I do to—to 'make it up to the kid'? I'm not a kid myself any longer, am I? I've no money, no special training, no husband! What's left for me? Sweeping floors! Washing dishes!"

"The only way that matters, to make it up to the kid," Ilse Kronstadt said, "is to love him."

"Oh, sure," Sarah Howson said bitterly. "What's that bit about 'flesh of my flesh, bone of my bone'? Don't preach at me. I had nothing but preaching from Gerald, and it got him a shot in the head and me a crippled boy to nurse. Can I go now? I've had enough."

The piercing blue eyes closed briefly, and the lids squeezed and the lips pressed together and the forehead drew down to furrows at the top of the sharp nose.

"Yes, you can go. There are too many people like you in the world for us to cure the world's sickness overnight. But even if you can't love the kid wholeheartedly, Miss Howson, you can at least remember that there was a time when you wanted a baby, for a reason you aren't likely to forget."

"He'll remind me every time I look at him," Sarah Howson said curtly, and got up from her chair. The officer reached for the phone again and spoke to a different number.

"Nurse, bring the Howson baby back to the lobby, please."

When the unwilling mother had gone, he gave Ilse Kronstadt a questioning glance.

"What was that about her grandfather?"

"Never mind," was the sighing answer. "There are a million problems like her's. I wish I could concern myself with all of them, but I just can't."

She became brisk. "At least the big problem is soluble. We should be out of here in another month, I guess."

iii

Things continued badly for a while longer. Stores remained closed; sporadic outbreaks confirmed that the thwarted terrorists were still capable of striking blindly, like children in tantrums. There were some fires, and the main city bridge was closed for two days by a plastic-bomb explosion.

Little by little calm oozed back. Sarah Howson made no attempt to chart its progress. There was news on TV when the broadcasting schedule was restored; there was also—had been, throughout the crisis—radio news. Sometimes she caught snatches of information: something about the new government, something else about advisers and foreign loans and public-welfare services. . . . It was beyond her scope. She saw black headlines on discarded newspapers when she went down the street, and read them without understanding. There was no association in her mind between the arrival of technical experts and the fact that water became available at her kitchen sink whenever she wanted it, as in the old days, rather than for two hours morning and evening, as during the "crisis." There was no connection that she could see between the new government and the cans of baby formula issued against coupons at the corner store, labeled in six languages and bearing a colored picture as well, for the benefit of illiterates.

It was agreed by everyone that things were worse now. In fact, from the material point of view things were slightly better. What depressed people so much was a subjective consideration. It had happened *here*. We, our families, our city, our country, have been shamed in the eyes of the world; murder was done on our streets, there were dynamite outrages and acts of terrorism *here*. Shame and self-condemnation turned readily to depression and apathy.

There was no true economic depression, and little unemployment, during the next few years, but some of the savor of life seemed to be missing. Fashions no longer changed so quickly and colorfully. Cars no longer sported startling decoration, but became functional and monotonous. People felt obscurely that to treat themselves to luxuries was a betrayal of—of *something;* as it were, they wanted to be seen to concentrate on the search for a new national goal, a symbol of status to redeem their world-watched failure.

Extravagance became a mark of social irresponsibility, the badge of the fringe criminal—the man with influence, the black-marketeer. These latter regarded the average run of the population—puritanical, working hard as though to escape a horrible memory—as mugs. The "mugs" condemned as parasites those who were blatantly enjoying themselves.

Through this epoch Sarah Howson moved like a sleepwalker, measuring her life by routine events. For a while there was some sort of an allowance, issued in scrip and redeemable at specified stores, which was just about enough to keep her and the child. She didn't bother to wonder about it, even though it was much discussed by ordinary folk: usually they condemned it, because it was available to women like Sarah Howson, who had committed the double crime of bearing an illegitimate child and also associating with a known terrorist. But these discussions she seldom heard; now hardly anyone talked to her in the street where she lived.

When the period of the allowance expired, she got work

for a while cleaning offices and serving at the counter of a canteen. Wages were low, part of the general syndrome of reaction against affluence which had followed the up-heaval. She hunted without much success for better-paid employment.

Then she met a widower with a teen-age son and daughter who wanted a housekeeper-mistress and didn't mind about the brat or her decaying looks. She moved across the city to his apartment in a large, crumbling near-tenement block and was at least secured against poverty. There was a roof and a bed, food, a little spending money for clothes, for the child, for a bottle of liquor on Satur-day night.

Young Gerald endured what happened to him without objection: being placed in a nursery while his mother worked as a cleaner, being put aside, like an inanimate object, at the widower's apartment when they moved there. At the nursery, naturally, they had clucked sympathetically about his deformity and made inquiries into his medical record, which was already long. But there was nothing to be done except exercise his limbs and enable him to make the best possible use of them. He learned to talk late, but quickly; surveying the world with bright grave eyes set in his idiot's face, he progressed from concrete to ab-stract concepts without difficulty, as though he had delayed speaking deliberately until he had thought the matter through.

But by then he was no longer being sent to the nursery, so no one with specialized knowledge noted this promis-ing development.

Crawling hurt him; he did it only for a short period, whimpering after a brief all-fours excursion like a dog with a thorn in its pad. He was four before he got his awkward limbs sufficiently organized to stand up without support, but he had already learned to get around a room with his hand on the wall or clutching chairs and tables. Once he could stand without toppling, he seemed almost to force himself to finish the job; swaying on slow, uneven legs, he set out into the middle of the room—fell—rose without complaint and tried again.

He would always limp, but at least when it came time for schooling he could walk a straight line, achieve a hobbling run for twenty yards, and climb stairs with alternate feet rather than using both feet for every step.

His mother's attitude was one of indifference by now. Here he was—a fact, to be endured. So there was no praise or encouragement when he mastered some difficult task such as the stairs—only a shrug of qualified relief that he wasn't totally helpless. The widower sometimes took him on his knee, told him stories, or answered questions for him, but showed no great enthusiasm for the job. He would excuse himself by saying he was too old to be much interested in young kids; after all, his own children were of an age to leave home, maybe to marry. But sometimes he was more honest, and confessed that the kid disturbed him. The eyes—maybe that was it: the bright eyes in the slack face. Or else it was the adult form of the sentences that emerged in the hesitant babyish voice.

When she was feeling more than usually tolerant of her son, Sarah Howson took him around the stores with her, defiantly accepting the murmurs of false pity which inevitably echoed around her. Here, in this part of the city, she wasn't known as Gerald Pond's mistress. But taking him out involved getting the folding wheelchair down the narrow, many-angled stairway of the apartment house, so she didn't do it often. Before she left to get married, the widower's daughter took him a few times to a children's park and put him on swings and showed him the animals kept there—a pony, rabbits, squirrels and bush babies. But the last time she tried it he sat silent, staring at the agility of the monkeys, and tears crawled down his cheeks.

There was TV in the apartment, and he learned early how to switch it on and change channels. He spent a great deal of time gazing at it, obviously not understanding a fraction of what was going on—and yet perhaps he did; it was impossible to be sure. One thing was definite, if surprising: before he started school, before he could read or write, he could be trusted to answer the phone and memorize a message flawlessly, even if it included a phone number of full cross-country direct-dialing length.

He had seen few books before he began school. Neither his mother nor the widower read for pleasure, though they took a daily paper. The son bought men's magazines for the spicy items and the nudes; the daughter bought fashion magazines occasionally, though the climate was still against excessive elegance, and romantic novels and love comics.

His first steps toward reading came from TV. He figured out for himself the sound-to-symbol idea, and school only filled in the details for him—he already had the outline. He progressed so rapidly that the teacher into whose care he was put came around to see his mother after six weeks. She was young and idealistic, and acutely conscious of the prevailing mood of the country.

She tried to persuade Sarah Howson that her son was too promising to be made to suffer the knocks and mockery of the other children in a regular school. The government had lately set up a number of special schools, one of them on the outskirts of the city, for children in need of unusual treatment. Why not, she demanded, arrange for his transfer?

Sarah Howson was briefly tempted, although she had visions of forms, applications, letters to write, interviews, appointments, all of which dismayed her. She inquired if he could be sent to the special school as a boarding pupil.

The teacher checked the regulations, and found the answer: No, not when the home was less than one hour's travel by public transport from the nearest such school. (Except as provided for in clause X, subsection Y, paragraph Z . . . and so on.)

Sarah Howson thought it over. And finally shook her head. She said, "Listen! You're pretty much of a kid yourself still. I'm not. Anything could happen to me. My man isn't going to want to be responsible for Gerry, is he? Not his kid! No, Gerrry has to learn to look after himself. It's a hard world, for God's sake! If he's as bright as you say, he'll make out. To my mind, he's got to. Sooner or later."

For a while thereafter, she did take more interest in him, though; she had vague visions that he wasn't going to be useless after all—support in old age, earn a decent living at some desk job. . . . But the habit wasn't there, and the interest declined.

There was trouble sometimes. There was taunting and

sometimes cruelty, and once he was made to climb a tree
under goading from a kids' gang and fell from a ten-foot
branch, a fall which luckily did no more than bruise him,
but the bruise was huge and remained tender for more
than three weeks. Seeing it, Sarah Howson had a sudden
appalling recollection of her meeting with the Israeli
woman, and firmly slapped down the memory.

There was also the time when he wouldn't go to school,
because of the torment he underwent. When he was escorted there to stop him from playing hooky, he refused
to cooperate in class; he drew faces on his books, or sat
gazing at the ceiling and pretended not to hear when he
was spoken to.

He got over that eventually. The mood of the city, and
the country, was changing. The trauma of the "crisis" was
receding, a litle joy was no longer suspect, frills and fun
were coming back into style. Relaxing, people were
more tolerant. He made his first friends when he was
about thirteen, at about the same time that local store-
keepers and housewives found that he was willing to limp
on errands or feed the cat when the family was away—
and could be trusted to complete the job, unlike other
boys, who might equally well decide to go to a movie with
the gang instead.

He was considering a career when the widower died.
He had vague thoughts of some job where his deformity
and other, newly discovered peculiarities were irrelevant.
But the widower died, and he was legally of age to quit
school.

And his mother was ill. It was some months before it
was known to be from inoperable cancer, but he had suspected it ever since the first symptoms. Before she was
ill enough to be hospitalized, he was having to support her
by what odd jobs he could find: making up accounts for
people, washing-up in a nearby bar and grill on Saturdays,
and such like. He had had little acquaintance with hope in
his life so far. By the time of his mother's death, which
left him alone at seventeen—ugly, awkward, a year lost
on the schooling which he had figured would continue to
college if he could get a public scholarship—he was
embittered.

He found a room a couple of blocks from the old apartment, which had been claimed by the municipal housing authority for a family with children. And kept going as he had been: with odd jobs for subsistence, with books and magazines, with TV when he could beg entrance to someone's home, and a movie occasionally when he had spare cash for escapism.

At twenty, Gerald Howson was convinced that the world which had been uncaring when he was born was uncaring now, and he spent as much time as possible withdrawing from it into a private universe where there was nobody to stare at him, nobody to shout at him for clumsiness, nobody to resent his existence because his form blasphemed the shape of humanity.

iv

The girl at the box office of the neighborhood movie theater knew him by sight. When he limped to join the waiting line, she made a kind of mental check mark, and his ticket was already clicking from the machine before he could ask for it; one for the cheapest seats, as always. He appreciated that. He was given to speaking rather little now, being so aware of the piping, immature quality of his voice.

Some few things about himself he had been able to disguise. His height, naturally, wasn't one of them. He had stopped growing at twelve, when he was barely five feet tall. But an old woman had taken pity on him a year back; she had formerly been a trained seamstress and worked in high-class tailor shops, and she got out her old needles and remade a jacket he had bought, setting shoulder pads into it and cunningly adjusting the hang of the back so that from the waist up he could pass a casual inspection. Also he had a high heel on the shoe of his shorter leg. It couldn't stop him from limping, because the leg still dragged slightly, but it gave him a better posture and seemed to lessen the endless ache from the muscles in the small of his back.

The jacket had been worn almost every day for a year, and was fraying, and the old woman was dead. He tried not to think about that. He went across the lobby to the kind darkness of the auditorium, with occasional snatched glances at the advertisements on the wall. Next week's show—the same as this, held over by public demand.

Consequently, with the house lights up and minutes still to go before the start of the program, there were many people to stare at him over popcorn-full mouths as he went down toward the base of the gigantic screen. He tried not to be aware of that, either.

The center front rows were all full of teen-age kids. He turned down a side aisle and went to an unoccupied end seat; the view of the screen would be badly angled, but it was that or a tedious business of stumbling over other people's feet, maybe treading on toes with his dragging shorter leg. He sat down and looked at the blank screen, his mind filling as always with fantasy images. The mere environment of the theater seemed to take him out of himself, even before the movie started. Snatches of conversation, pictures, moods of elation and depression, all flickered past his atttention, and brought a sense of taut excitement. Some of the material in this mental variety show could startle him with its unfamiliarity, but he had always assumed it was due to his surroundings provoking a recurrence of otherwise forgotten memory. He had seen hundreds of movies here; they must be the source of the ideas crowding his mind.

And yet . . . that wasn't too satisfying as an explanation, somehow.

A man in brown came striding down the main aisle, all the way to the front, turned sharply toward the side where Howson sat, took the seat diagonally in front of him, and threw an overcoat across the seat adjacent. He shrugged aside his sleeve and stared at his watch before leaning back and turning his head toward the screen.

That, or the fact that he was well-dressed, and should by appearance have been in the expensive seats, or something not available to consciousness, attracted Howson's attention to him. For no definable reason, he was sure the man in brown hadn't consulted his watch simply to know how much time remained before show time. The man was not . . . not exactly nervous, but on edge about something, and it wasn't the prospect of a good movie.

His puzzlement was cut short by the darkening of the auditorium, and he forgot everything except the huge colored images parading across the screen. By night and day his dreams were populated from movies, TV and magazines; he preferred movies because his fellow watchers didn't care about his presence, and although people were willing enough to let him sit and see their TV, there was always that tense awkwardness.

Besides, with every breath he seemed to draw in the enjoyment of the rest of the audience, adding it to his own.

First, a travelogue, *Playgrounds of the Planet*. The crashing music of surf at Bondi Beach, the humming roar of turbine cars as they streaked down the Sahara Highway, the whish and whir of skis on an Alpine slope and then the yammer of pulse-jet skimmers on blue Pacific water. Howson shut his ears to the syrupy wise-cracking commentator. He made his own commentary, as though he could shift personalities like shifting gears, choosing a hard-boiled masculine frame of mind for admiring the next-to-nude girls at Bondi, a worried near-feminine attitude for the ski-jumpers—thoughts of pain on failure, bruises, broken bones. . . . He shied away from the recollection of a tree he had fallen out of.

So all through. But the cars lingered longest. To be on the Sahara Highway, knife-cut-straight for two hundred miles at a stretch, where there was no limping; the photo-reactive glass of the roof automatically darkened against the harsh sun, the counter of the turbine steady at its two hundred thousand revs, the gangs of dark-skinned men at work with the sand-sweeps, one every ten miles, the glimpses of artificial oases islanded by sand, where with water and tough grass and mutated conifers men struggled to reclaim once-fertile land—that was a dream to cherish.

Advertisements. Coming attractions. His mind wandered, and his attention centered briefly on the man in brown, who was checking his watch again and gazing around as though expecting someone. Girl friend? Somehow not. Howson let the problem slide as the main titles of the big feature sprang into red life on the screen.

Howson knew little about his father; he had learned tact early because it was the complement, as it were, of the treatment he received at school, so scraps of information put together had to take the place of direct questioning of his mother. He still knew scarcely anything about the political crisis that had gestated along with him, and its worst after effects were over by the time he became aware of such things as news and international affairs.

Even so, he sensed something special about movies of this kind. He couldn't analyze what led to the reaction of audiences watching them, but he knew he liked the feeling; everyone seemed to be cautiously self-conscious, as though he were testing out a leg fresh from surgical splints, and establishing by the absence of expected pain that it would take his full weight.

In a way, that parallel was exact. The trauma of the "crisis" had subsided to such a degree that it would soon be possible to teach children about it, treating it as history. Experience had persuaded those who recalled it clearly that it wasn't the end of everything: here was life going on, and the country was prosperous, and children were growing up happy, and worry had proved needless.

So now the movie theaters were full when there was a picture like this one playing—and there were lots like this one, and Howson had seen several. Absurd, spectacular, violent, melodramatic, they always centered on terrorism or war-prevention in some colorful corner of the world, and their heroes were the mysterious, half-understood agents of the UN who read minds—the honorable spies, the telepathists.

Here now the story was a romance. Clean-cut, tall, good-looking mind-reading agent encounters blond, tall, beautiful, sadly misled mind-reading girl maintained under hypnosis by fanatical group bent on blowing up a nuclear-power station in the furtherance of their greed for conquest. The older members of the audience squirmed a little under the impact of too-familiar images: olive-green trucks thundering down a moonlit road, soldiers deploying unhurriedly around the main intersections of a big city, an abandoned child weeping as it wandered through silent alleys.

There were obvious attempts to parallel reality at certain points, but not many. There was, for instance, a motherly Jewish woman telepathist intended to resemble the legendary Ilse Kronstadt; in the front rows of the audience, teenage girls who had let their boys' hands wander too intimately across their breasts squirmed under the horrible but delicious idea that real mothers should read this memory from them later—horrible for the expected row to follow, delicious for the hope that parents were indeed ultimately dependable.

And the boys wondered about being telepathic, and thought of knowing for sure whether the girls would or wouldn't—and power, and money.

Meantime, Howson. It didn't seem to him especially insightful to realize that it couldn't actually happen this way; for him, this fictionalization was on the same footing as a camera trick, something to be taken on its own terms, with its own artificial logic. His fantasies and his real environment were too unalike to become confused in his mind.

His genetic handicap had at least spared him any obsession with sexuality, and he was diffusely grateful that he had no intolerable yearnings which his appearance would bar from fulfillment. But he did hunger for acceptance, and made the most of such crumbs of conversation as were thrown to him.

Accordingly he thought about these telepathists from a different standpoint: as persons set apart by a mental, rather than a physical, abnormality. He was sufficiently cynical to have realized that the admiration for telepathists provoked by this movie, by others like it, by official news stories, was artificial. Telepathists were elsewhere people, remote, wonderful, like snow on distant mountains. The thought of being able to pry secrets from other people's minds appealed to this audience around him, no matter how carefully the dialogue and action skirted the point, the instant the corollary presented itself—the idea of having *your* mind invaded—there was a violent revulsion. The ambivalence was omnipresent: consciously one could know that telepathists were saving life, saving sanity, guiding countries (like this one) away from war— and yet it made no difference to the instinctual alarm.

Their existence had been eased into public consciousness with shoehorn care: rumors purposely allowed to run wild to the point of absurdity had been deflated by calm official announcements rendered believable by sheer contrast; quiet ceremonies made small items for news bulletins—such-and-such a telepathist working for the UN was today decorated with the highest order of such-and-such a country recently saved from civil war. For the real people behind the public image one might hunt indefinitely, and end up with no more than a few names, a few blurred photographs, and some inexact secondhand information.

There was a policy behind even such far-out melodrama as this movie, Howson was sure. And for that reason, he was envious. He knew beyond doubt that the uncushioned impact of their abnormality on ordinary people would have culminated in persecution, maybe pogroms. But because the telepathists were important, the impact *was* cushioned—the world's resources were marshalled to help them.

He felt achingly the desire to be at least a little important, so that his deformity—no more extraordinary than a telepathist's mental peculiarities—would seem less catastrophic.

His mind wandered from the screen and was caught by the man in brown, who was no longer alone. His head was bent toward another man, who had sat down, without Howson realizing it, in the seat over which the man in brown had first thrown his topcoat. Searching back in memory, Howson realized he had seen the door of the men's room swing twice within the past few minutes.

He listened out of curiosity, and was suddenly sweating. He caught mumbled phrases, and pieced the rest together.

"*Boat on the river . . . two* A.M. *at Black Wharf*

. . . Cudgels has a personal stake in this lot . . . worth a good half-million, I'd say . . . little diversion for The Snake, keep his men busy other side of town . . . no problem with fuzz, bought the sergeant off . . ."

The men grinned at each other. The latecomer got up and went back into the men's room; before he returned and headed to his former seat elsewhere in the theater, the man in brown had put his topcoat over his arm and headed for the exit. Howson sat frozen, the chance of being important handed to him at the very moment when he was wishing for it.

Cudgels . . . The Snake: yes, it was certain. He'd never mixed in such business, but you couldn't live in this broken-down quarter of the city without hearing those names occasionally and learning that they were gang bosses and rivals. A club would be smashed up, a store's biggest plate-glass window broken, a young tough carried to the hospital from an alley lined with garbage cans and floored with his blood. Then one heard mention of Cudgels Lister and Horace "Snake" Hampton. Also a car would be pointed out by a knowing youth: "The smart way to the top; I'm going that way one day!"

Painfully, to the accompaniment of hard breathing, Howson forced himself to the crucial decision.

v

The street was still called Grand Avenue, but it had been one of the focal points of the crisis period. Afterwards people shied away from it, beginning the decline which had now reduced the side streets nearby to a status barely above slums. Even so, it was well lighted, and the garish stores had glaring windows, and Howson would normally have avoided it. He preferred the darker side of any street, and night to day.

Now, heart hammering, he braved it. There was a place at the far end—a club and bar—which served as the Snake's front for tax and other purposes. It was no use trying to make his ill-formed face look severe for the menacing encounter he was bound to; a mirror on the door of a barber's told him that as he passed. The best he could hope to do would be to look . . . well . . . casual.

The hell. It was what he had to say that mattered.

He hobbled clear past his destination the first time, because his mouth was so dry and his guts were so tense. He stopped a few yards farther on, and deliberately evened his breathing until he had some semblance of control. Then he plunged.

The bar was chromed, mirrored, neoned. Music blasted from speakers high on the wall. At tables early drinkers were grouped in twos and threes, but there was no one at the bar yet. A bored bartender leaned on his elbows and eyed the short stranger with the limp.

He said, "What'll it be?"

Howson didn't drink, had never tried alcohol. He'd seen shambling drunks and wondered why the hell anyone gifted with ordinary physical control should want to throw it away. The thought of being even more uncoordinated filled him with disgust. In any case, he had no spare money.

He said, "Is . . . uh . . . Mr. Hampton here?"

The bartender took his elbows off the counter. He said, "What's that to you, Crooky? He's not for public show!"

"I have something he'll want to hear," Howson said, mentally cursing the reedy pipe which had to serve him for a voice.

"He knows everything he wants to know," the bartender said curtly. "There's the door. Use it."

He picked up a damp cloth and began to swab beer rings off the bar.

Howson looked around and licked his lips. The customers had decided not to stare at him any more. Encouraged, he went the sidewise pace necessary to confront the bartender again.

"It's about some business of Cudgels'," he whispered.

His whisper was better than his ordinary voice—less distinctive.

"Since when did Cudgels tell you his stories?" the bartender said sourly. But he thought it over, and after a pause gave a shrug. Reaching under the bar, he seemed to grope for something—a buzzer, maybe. Shortly, a door behind the bar opened and a man with oily black hair appeared.

"Crooky here," the barman said. "Wants to sell news about Cudgels to Mr. Hampton."

The oily-haired man stared unbelievingly at Howson. Then he too shrugged, gestured; the flap of the bar was raised for Howson to limp through.

In back was the stockroom of the bar. Oily-hair escorted Howson through here, through a door lined with red baize, down a badly lighted corridor to a similar door. And beyond that, sat him down in a room furnished with four identical red velvet lounges, decorated with gilt pillars and pretty abstract paintings.

"Wait," Oily-hair said curtly, and went out.

Howson sat, very tense, on the edge of the velvet cushions, eyes roving as he tried to figure out what went on back here. He fancied he caught a clicking noise, and recalled a shot from a favorite movie. Roulette. The air smelled of anxiety, and that would be why.

Soon Oily-hair returned, beckoned him, and this time took him into a businesslike office where a lean man with pale hands presided behind a telephone-laden desk, tall youths like guards at either side of him. At Howson's entrance the looks on their faces changed; they had been wary, and became astonished.

Looking at the man behind the desk, Howson could see why he was called The Snake. His mere presence was devious; cunning lighted the dark irises of his eyes.

He studied Howson for a long moment, then lifted an eyebrow in wordless inquiry to Oily-hair.

"Crooky here wants to sell information about Cudgels," was the condensed explanation. "That's all I know."

"Hmmm . . . " The Snake rubbed his smooth chin. "And walks in unannounced. Interesting. Who are you, Crooky?"

It didn't seem to be as unkindly meant as it usually

was; it was simply a label. Maybe a man who was called The Snake was casual about such things. Howson cleared his throat.

"My name's Gerry Howson," he said. "I was down the movie theater an hour back. There was this guy waiting for someone to move to the next seat while the picture was playing. They whispered together, and I overheard them."

"Uh-huh," The Snake commented. "So-o-o?"

"This is where we get to the price," Oily-hair suggested.

"Shut up, Collar," The Snake said. He kept his eyes on Howson.

"A boat's coming upriver to Black Wharf at two A.M. I don't know for sure it's tonight, but I think so. It has half a million worth of stuff on it."

Howson waited, thinking belatedly that Collar was probably right—he should have named a price, at least, or fed the news by stages. Then he caught himself. No, he'd done it the right way. There was total silence. And it was lasting.

"So *that's* how he does it," The Snake said finally. "Hear that, Collar? Well, if you heard it, what are you doing standing there?"

Collar gulped audibly and snatched at one of the phones on the desk. There was another silence, during which the two guards stared with interest at Howson.

"Gizmo?" Collar said in a low voice to the phone. "Collar. You can talk? . . . General call. We have some night work . . . Yes, OK. Not more than two hours. Smooth!"

He cradled the phone. The Snake was getting to his feet. The process appeared to be complete. Howson felt a stab of panic at its speed. He said, "Uh, I guess it's worth something, isn't it?"

"Possibly." The Snake gave him a sleepy smile. "We'll know soon enough, won't we? Right now what it's worth is —oh, let's say a few drinks, a square meal, which you look like you could do with, and some company. Hear me, Lots?"

One of the youthful guards nodded and stepped forward.

"Look after him. He may be valuable, he may not: we'll see. Dingus!"

The other guard responded.

"He says his name is Gerry Howson. Get his address off him. Go down around where he lives and put some questions. Don't take more than a couple of hours over it. If you get the slightest smell—if anyone says he's even been seen on the same bus with one of Cudgels' boys—blow in and warn me. And sound out the fuzz on your way if you can find one of our friends on duty at headquarters."

Howson, fighting terror, said huskily, "This man in brown . . . he said he bought the sergeant, whichever that one is."

"He would. You didn't know either of these men, did you?" The Snake added, struck by the thought.

"No, I . . . uh . . . never saw them before."

"Mm-hm. All right, Lots, take him in the Blue Room and keep him there till Dingus gets back."

Lots wasn't unfriendly, Howson found; he dropped enough hints to make it clear that if the news he'd brought was true, it would plug a gap in The Snake's monopoly of some illegal goods or other—exactly what, Howson didn't ask. He fancied it might be drugs. His reaction of disgust against alcohol carried over to drugs, and he preferred not to pursue that line of thought. All he cared about was being momentarily of importance.

He sat with Lots in the Blue Room—decorated with a midnight blue ceiling and a heavy blue carpet—and told himself that it was only sense on the part of The Snake to make sure before he acted. Desultorily, he answered questions.

"What's your trouble from, Crooky?" Lots inquired. "Hurt in an accident?"

"Born like it," Howson said. Then the idea occurred to him that Lots was trying to be sympathetic, and he added in a tone of apology, "I don't talk about it much."

"Mm-hah." Lots yawned and stretched his legs straight out. "Drink? Or that meal The Snake said you were to have?"

"I don't drink," Howson said. Again he felt the rare

impulse to explain. "It isn't easy to walk when I'm sober, if you see what I mean."

Lots stared at him. After a moment he laughed harshly. "I don't guess I could make a crack like that, with your problem. OK, take a cola or something. I'm buzzing for gin."

There were crawling hours. Talk ceased after the food was brought. Lots proposed a game of stud, offered to teach the rules to him, changed his mind on seeing that Howson's awkward fingers couldn't cope with the task of dealing one card at a time. Embarrassed, Howson suggested chess or checkers, but Lots wasn't interested in either.

Eventually the door swung open and Dingus put his head in.

"Move it, Lots!" he exclaimed. "The guy checks out clean so far as we can tell. We're going to Black Wharf now."

Automatically Howson made to pull himself to his feet. With a sharp gesture Dingus stopped him.

"You still wait, Crooky!" he snapped. "Mr. Hampton's a hard man to satisfy, and there's a while yet till two A.M."

It felt more like an age dragging by when he was alone. At last, sometime after midnight, he dozed off in his chair. He had no idea how long he had slept when he was jolted awake by the door opening again. His bleary eyes focused on The Snake, and Lots and Dingus and Collar following him into the room. But the instant he saw them he knew his gamble had succeeded.

"You earned your pay, Crooky," The Snake said softly. "You surely did. Which leaves only one question."

Howson's mind, still sleep-fogged, groped for it. Would it be: how much did he want? The guess was wrong. The Snake continued, "And that is, are you an honest politician?"

Howson made a noncommittal noise. His mouth was dry with excitement again. The Snake looked him over thoughtfully for long seconds, and reached his decision. He snapped his fingers at Collar.

"Make it five hundred!" he instructed. "And—listening, Crooky?—remember that half of that is for the next time, if there is one. Lots, book out a car and take him home."

The shock of being given more money than he had ever held in his hand at one time before broke the barrier separating Howson's fantasies from reality; he barely absorbed the impressions of the next half hour—the car, the journey to his rooming house—because of the swarming visions that filled his mind. Not just next time: a time after that, and another and another, piecing gossip together into news, being paid, being (which was infinitely more important) praised and eventually regarded as valuable. That was what he wanted most in all the world. He had achieved what to almost anyone else would be a minor ambition; he had done something for someone which was not made work, offered out of sympathy, but original with himself. It was a milepost in memory because he had regarded it as impossible, like walking down the street without a limp.

That was the early morning of a Tuesday. His delirium and hope were fed for a few days by scraps of news and gossip: it was reported that there had been some kind of battle, and the police had cleared up the traces but were mystified by the details. It was as though he drew courage like oxygen from the atmosphere of rumor and tension; he went down Grand Avenue in full daylight, in the middle of the sidewalk instead of skulking to the wall, and could ignore the usual pitying stares because he knew inside himself what he was worth. With what seemed to him great cunning, he had changed his five hundred a long bus ride distant from his home and taken small bills, which would not excite comment; then he had hidden the bulk of them in his room and spent only as much as would get him a new pair of shoes with the unequal heels, a new jacket with the uneven shoulder pads.

Even so, on Saturday night his glorious new world fell apart in shards.

vi

*E*arly in the evening he had taken five singles from the concealed hoard in his room. He had never thought of spending so much on one spree before; often, after paying room rent, he would have no more than five left to carry him through a week. Then he was driven to his least-preferred resource: washing cutlery at a nearby diner to earn plates of unwanted scraps. Cutlery didn't break when he dropped it; cups and glasses did, so the owner no longer let him wash those. And the knowledge that this was given to him as a favor hurt badly.

Tonight, though, he was going the limit. A movie he hadn't seen; Cokes, candy, ices, all the childish treats he still preferred to anything else. Mostly he was self-conscious about really liking them, but in his present mood he could achieve defiance. The hell with what people might think about a twenty-year-old who craved candy and ices!

He wished that the new jacket and shoes could have been ready by now, but he had been told they would take at least ten days. So nothing for it but to get a shine for the dulled leather, brush awkwardly at the dirty marks on the cloth.

And then out: a Saturday night and a good time, something to make him feel halfway normal, an action ordinary people took.

Down the narrow street where folks knew him, looked at him without the shock of surprise, maybe called a hello—but tonight not, strangely enough. But his mind was preoccupied, and he didn't spare the energy to wonder why there were no spoken greetings. He had the distinct impression that people were thinking about him, but that was absurd, a byproduct of his elation.

Yet the impression wouldn't leave him. Even when he had braved the lights of Grand Avenue and was moving among crowds of strangers, his mind kept presenting it afresh, like a poker dealer demonstrating his ability to deal complete suits one after another.

At first it was amusing. After a while it began to irritate him. He changed his mind about taking in the early-evening show at the movie theater of his choice—not his regular one, which was still playing the program he had seen, but one he had to get to by bus. The public's mood was good tonight, and somebody had helped him board the bus, making other people stand back, but even that didn't improve his state of mind. More, it was an annoying emphasis on his state of body.

And at last, an hour and a half after setting out, he was so disturbed that he had to abandon his plan. Instead, he turned homeward, furious with himself, thinking it was lack of guts that spoiled his enjoyment, and determined to convince himself it was an illusion which plagued him.

As he neared the street where he lived, the feeling grew stronger, for all his attempts to deny it. It was as if he was being watched. Once he halted abruptly and swung around, sure somebody's eyes were fixed on him. There was no one in the place where he looked by reflex; he was staring at a closed door. While he was still bewildered, the door opened and a girl came out, pausing and glancing back to say something to a person inside the house.

From that moment on the sensation pounded at his skull. Dizzily he kept moving, and tried to evade the concept which had crawled from a dark corner of his brain to leer at him. He failed. It took form in sluggish words.

I'm going insane. I must be going insane.

He turned the corner of his own street, and put his hand on the rough concrete wall to steady himself and gulp air. And then he knew.

Ahead of him, standing at his own door, was a large white car, its roof decorated with a flashing beacon, its nose with a sign saying POLICE. A driver leaned his elbow casually on his lowered window; two uniformed officers were bending together to speak to him.

He could hear them. They were fifty yards away; they were talking barely above a whisper, and he knew every word that passed because they were discussing him.

"*Out right now . . . Goes to movies mostly . . . Might be doing something for The Snake. . . . Unlikely; new on his payroll, the story is . . . Must have gone to The Snake first; The Snake doesn't go shopping for help . . .*"

Mortal terror welled up in Howson's mind. A car jolted around the corner, and before the turn was complete he had fled, with the impossible voices in pursuit, like ghosts.

"*Ask at the neighborhood movie theater . . . Not worth the trouble, is it? Unless someone warned him off, he'll be back eventually. Wait in his room, or pick him up in the small hours . . .*"

Aimed at him—aimed at *me*, Gerald Howson: as the forces of all the world had been leveled at this city the day of my birth!

But that was only half the reason for his terror. The other and worse half was knowing what he had become. He *could not* have heard what the policemen were saying so far away. Yet the words had reached him, and they had been colored by what was not exactly a tone of voice but was nonetheless individual: a tone of *thought*. One tone was ugly; the thinker had a streak of brutality, and liked the power his uniform implied. He envisaged beating. They said cripple; so what? He'd been responsible for a death, for a gang fight, for crime. So beat him into talking.

Howson couldn't face the shock in simple terms: *I am a telepathist*. It came to him in the form he had conceived when watching the movie about telepathists: *I am abnormal mentally as well as physically*.

Had he even overheard what the man in brown was telling his seat neighbor? Or had he then, already, picked up thought?

He couldn't tackle that question. He was in flight, hobbling into the hoped-for anonymity of a crowd, wanting to go as far and as fast as he could, not capable of halting

for a bus because to stand still when he was hunted was
intolerable. His eyes blurred, his legs hurt, his lungs
pumped, straining volumes of air, and he lost all contact
with deliberate planning. Merely to move was the maximum he could manage.

Toward what future was he stumbling now? Every
looming building seemed to tower infinitely high above
his head, making unclimbable canyons out of the familiar
streets; every lamp-eyed car seemed to growl at him like
a tracking hound; every intersection presaged a colli-
sion with doom, so that he was sickened by relief when
he saw that there were not roadblocks around each
successive corner. His ears rang, his muscles screamed—
and he kept on.

His direction was random; he followed as nearly as
possible the straight line dictated by his home street. It
took him through a maze of grimy residential roads, then
through a district of warehouses and light industry where
signs reported paper-cup-making and tailoring and plastic-
furniture-making. Late trucks nosed down those streets,
and he knew the drivers noticed him and was afraid, but
could do nothing to escape their sight.

The district changed again; there were small stores, bars,
music bellowing, TV sets playing silently in display windows to an audience of steam irons and fluorescent lamps.
He kept moving.

Then, abruptly, there were blank walls, twelve feet
high, in gray concrete and dusty red brick. He halted,
thinking confusedly of prison, and turned at hazard to the
right. In a while he realized where he had come to; he
was close to the big river up which Cudgels had tried to
sneak his half-million worth of—of whatever it was.
Signs warned him that this was EAST MAIN DOCK BONDING
ZONE FOR DUTIABLE GOODS and there was NO ADMISSION
WITHOUT AUTHORITY OF CHIEF CUSTOMS INSPECTOR.

The idea of "authority" blended with his confused
images of police hounding him. He changed direction
frantically, and struck off down a twisting alley, away from
the high imprisoning wall. In all his life he had never
driven himself so hard; the pain in his legs was almost un-
endurable. And here there was a fearful silence, not
heard with the ears, but experienced directly: whole block-

sized areas empty of people, appalling to Howson, the city child, who had never slept more than twenty feet from another person.

The alley was abruptly only half an alley. The wall on his left ended, and there was bare ground enclosed with wire on wooden poles. He blinked through semidarkness, for there were few lamps. The promise of haven beckoned: the waste ground was the site of a partly demolished warehouse, the rear section of which still stood. Hung on the wire, smeared with thrown filth, were weathered boards: FOR SALE—PURCHASER TO COMPLETE DEMOLITION.

He grubbed along the base of the wire fence like a snuffling animal, seeking a point of entry. He found one, where children, presumably, had uprooted a post and pushed it aside. Uncaring that he was smearing himself with mud by crawling through the gap, he twisted under the wire and made his way to the shelter of the ruin.

As he fell into the lee of a jagged wall, his exhaustion, shock and terror mingled, and a wave of blackness gave him release.

His waking was fearful, too. It was the first time in his life that he saw, on waking, without opening his eyes, and the first time he saw himself.

The circuit of consciousness closed, and muddy images came to him, conflicting with the evidence of his familiar senses. He felt stiff, cold; he knew his weight and position, flat on his back on a pile of dirty old sacks, his head raised a little by something rough and unyielding. Simultaneously he knew gray half-light, an awkward, twisted form like a broken doll with a slack face—his own, seen from outside. And blended with all this, he was aware of wrong physical sensations: of level shoulders, which he had never had, and of something heavy on his chest, but pulling down and forward—another deformity?

Then he understood, and cried out, and opened his eyes, and fright taught him how to withdraw from an unsought mental link. He struck out and found his hands tangled in a rope of greasy hair, a foot away from him.

A stifled moan accompanied his attempt to make sense of his surroundings. He hadn't fallen on his back when he passed out; certainly he hadn't fallen on this makeshift bed: so he had been put there. And this would be the person responsible: this girl kneeling at his side, with the coarse, heavy face, thick arms, wide, scared eyes.

Scared of me! Never before was anyone scared of me!

But even as he prepared savagely to enjoy the sensation, he discovered that he couldn't. The sense of fear was like a bad smell in his nostrils. Convulsively he let go the tress of hair he had seized, and the fear diminished. He pushed himself into a sitting position, looking the girl over.

She appeared to be about sixteen or seventeen, although her face was not made up as was customary by that age. She was blockily built, poorly clothed in a dark-gray coat over a thin cotton dress; the garments were clean, but her hands were muddy from the ground.

"Who are you?" Howson said thickly. "What do you want?"

She didn't answer. Instead, she reached quickly to one side and picked up a paper bag, turning it so that he could see through the mouth of it. Inside there were crusts of bread, a chunk of cheese, two bruised apples. Puzzled, Howson looked from the food to her face, wondering why she was gesturing to him, moving her thick lips in a pantomime of eating but not saying anything.

Then, as though in despair, she uttered a thick bubbling sound, and he understood.

Oh, God! You're deaf and dumb!

Wildly she dropped the bag of food and jumped to her feet, her brain seething with disbelief. She had sensed his thought, projected by his untrained telepathic "voice," and the total strangeness of the feeling had rocked her already ill-balanced mind on its foundations. Once more the sickening odor of fear colored Howson's awareness, but this time he knew what was happening, and his uncontrolled wave of pity for such another as himself, crippled in a heedless world, reached her also.

Incontinently she dropped to her knees again, this time letting her head fall forward and starting to sob. Uncertainly he put out his hand. She clutched it violently, and a tear splashed, warm and wet, on his fingers.

He registered another first time in his life now. As best he could, he formulated a deliberate message, and let it pass the incomprehensible channel newly opened in his mind. He tried to say *Don't be afraid,* and then *Thank you for helping me,* and then *You'll get used to me talking to you.*

Waiting to see if she understood, he stared at the crown of her head as though he could picture there the strange and dreadful future to which he was condemned.

vii

*W*hen he thought it over later, he saw that that first simple attempt at communication had by itself implied his future. His instinctive reaction stemmed from his disastrous and unique essay in making himself significant; he had snatched with panic at the chance of passing on news to The Snake, with no more thought of consequences than a starving man falling on a moldy crust. Arriving simultaneously with his recognition that he was a telepath, the shock of realizing that he had made himself by definition a criminal—an accessory to murder, to be precise—had swung the compass needle of his intentions through a semicircle. He wanted nothing so much as to escape back to obscurity, and the idea of being a telepathist appalled him. Challenged during his terror-stricken flight down darkened streets, he would have sworn that he wanted never to use the gift.

As well declare the intention to be deaf forever! Eyes might be kept shut by an effort of will, but this thing which had come to him was neither sight, nor hearing, nor touch; it was incomparable, and inevitable.

The sensation was giddying at first. It drew from memory forgotten phrases, in which he sought guidance and reassurance: from a long-ago class in school, something about "men as trees walking"—that was curiously meaningful. His problem was multiplied tenfold by the puzzling, abnormal world in which the girl had spent her life, and paradoxically it was also simplified, because the more he learned about the handicap she labored under, the more he came to consider himself lucky. Faced with Howson as a cripple, people might still come to see there was a *person* inside the awkward shell. But the deaf-and-dumb girl had never been able to convey more than basic wants, using finger code, so people regarded her as an animal.

Her brain was entire; the lack was in the nerves connecting ears and brain, and in the form of her vocal cords, which were so positioned that they could never vibrate correctly, but only slap loosely together to give a bubbling grunt. Yet it seemed to Howson she should have been helped. He knew of special training schemes reported in newspapers and on TV. Groping, he hunted for the reasons why not.

At first he could make no sense of the impressions he took from her mind, because she had never developed verbal thinking; she used kinesthetic and visual data in huge intermingled blocks, like a sour porridge with stones in it. While he struggled to achieve more than the first broad halting concepts of reassurance, she sat gazing at him and weeping silently released from loneliness after intolerable years, too overcome to question the mode of their communication.

The clue he sought came when he tried to reinterpret the things he had "said" to her. He had "said": *Don't be afraid,* and she had formulated the concept into familiar images, half memory, half physical sensations of warmth and satisfaction that traced clear back to infantile experiences at the breast. He had "said": *Thank you for helping me,* and there were images of her parents smiling. Those were rare. Struggling, he pursued them to find what her life had been like.

There was a peculiar doubling in the areas he explored next. Half the girl's mind knew what her father was actually like: a dockland roustabout, always dirty, often drunk, with a filthy temper and a mouth that gaped terrifyingly, uttering *something* which she compared to an invisible vomit because she had never heard a single word spoken. Much to Howson's surprise, she was quite aware of the function of normal speech; it was only this rage-driven bellowing of her father that she regarded thus.

But at the same time as she saw her father for what he was, she maintained an idealized picture of him, blended out of the times when he had dressed smartly for weddings and parties, and the times when he had shown loving behavior toward her as his daughter, not as a useless burden. And this image was still further overlaid with traces of an immense fantasy from whose fringes Howson shied away reflexively, in the depths of which the girl was a foundling princess.

Her mother was barely remembered; she had got lost at some stage of the girl's childhood, and had been replaced by a succession of women of all ages from twenty to fifty, their relationship to her father and herself ill-comprehended. They came and went from the tenement house her father rented, in a pattern she could not fathom because she could not speak to ask the necessary questions.

Out of this background of dirt, frustration and deprivation of affection, she had conceived a need which Howson understood instantly because it paralleled his own desire for importance. Even though it had blown up in his face, he still yearned. But the girl yearned for a key to the mystery of speech, the glass door shutting her off from everybody. In a frantic attempt to substitute some other link for this missing one, she had developed the habit of spending all her time helping, or working for, nearby families; a smile of thanks for minding a baby, or a small payment for running an errand simple enough to explain by signs, was her only emotional sustenance.

Lately she had needed this support more than ever; her father had drunk so much he had been warned off his job until he sobered up—at least, that was how Howson interpreted the ill-detailed memories available to his investigations. As a result, he had been more violent and bad-tempered than ever, and his daughter had to stay out of the house to avoid him until he was asleep. Finding Howson when she came to the half-ruined warehouse to hide from the wind, she had helped him automatically —making him comfortable on the pile of old sacks, going in search of food for him, in the hope of a little praise and gratitude.

He reached that stage of his fumbling inquiry, and grew aware that his head was aching. The exercise of his new faculty wasn't difficult in itself; it was perhaps like seeing a picture for the first time, when the shapes and colors were available to vision just by looking, and what had to be learned was a set of rules for matching them to solid objects already known, using enlightened guesswork. On the other hand, it was tiring to concentrate so long. He began to withdraw contact.

Sensing his intention, the girl shot out her hand and seized his, her eyes wide and pleading. Blazing in her mind, unverbalized but impossible to misconstrue, was a desperate appeal.

The memory of near-disaster, still only a few hours old, was far too fresh for Howson to have conceived any new ambitions. He had no notion of what he wanted to do with his developing talent; using it was giving him a sense of giddy, fearful excitement, like steering a fast car for the first time, and that was all he could think about as yet. His instinct still warned him that he should seek obscurity for fear of consequences.

Yet, here was the chance he craved to be important to somebody. Not much of a somebody, true: just a deprived, unhappy, physically handicapped girl in a plight resembling his own.

It was too early to decide which of these opposing tugs would eventually win out, but for the moment at any rate he had no alternative plan to granting the girl's desire: *Be with me!*

She chuckled, a thick, inhuman sound, and gave a wide grin, and caught up the forgotten bag of food to force it into his hand and make him eat.

Uncounted, time slipped by. It seemed to carry him forward by simple inertia. Things were done, as he grew accustomed to a fugitive existence; by night there were furtive expeditions in search of food, when his telepathic gift gave warning of anyone approaching and there was time to dodge out of sight, and by day there were tasks in plenty which he could not have attempted by himself.

Hidden behind a low wall of the old warehouse, a sort of crude lean-to took shape. As unquestioning as a dog, the girl brought old planks and rusty nails and found rocks to use as hammers. She was stronger than Howson, of course. Almost anyone was stronger than he was.

She never left him after their original encounter. Her father was a shred of mist compared to the presence of Howson, who could actually communicate with her; the mere idea of separation from him for longer than a few minutes terrified her, implying a permanent return to her old loneliness. At first he was worried that someone would come looking for her. Then he decided the risk was negligible, and turned his attention to his own problems.

He spent long hours in silent contemplation, his mind clouded with misery, thinking of all the money he had briefly had, now hidden in his old room and impossible to recover; of his new jacket and shoes, which he dared not go to fetch. How long it would be before he could venture back on the streets, he couldn't tell. Once or twice he picked up the stray thoughts of a patrolling policeman, and knew there was still a description of him being circulated.

This squalid, vegetable existence which was all he felt safe in allowing himself began to prey on him after a few days. Since he could not escape from it physically, he evaded it mentally, daydreaming after the old fashion but trying to fit his new gift into the scheme.

The movies about telepathists which he had seen provided a ready-made frame to work with. Curious, he inquired of the girl as to her enjoyment of movies and TV, and found what he expected—that the stories mattered little to her, since she could hardly follow them without the dialogue, but that the color and glamour obsessed her.

Tentatively, borrowing from her own long-time fantasy about the rich father and adoring mother who would come to claim their long-lost child and bring the gift of speech, he tried to make it clear what she had been missing by not hearing anything. As they huddled together for warmth in their drafty shed of a home, he elaborated huge mental dramas, where he was tall, straight-backed, handsome, and where she was fine-featured, shapely, glamorously dressed.

The real, cruel world began to seem less and less important; the little he saw of it was drabber than ever. He came slowly to feel that if it never again had any truck with him, he would be happy. Occasionally he recalled that telepathists were well treated by that world, praised and highly valued. But he couldn't be sure that there were no other consequences of presenting himself for the attention of authority. He considered going to officials and saying, "I'm a telepathist!" He reconsidered it, and postponed the day. Meanwhile, there was a world of dreams to engage his interest, and daily the dreams grew brighter and more elaborate.

Yet, all the time he was hiding from the world, he was telling the world about himself.

The communications man fastened the helmet to the ring around his neck, closing himself off from the universe by all normal sensory channels. Blind, deaf, weightlessly suspended, he let himself be sealed into the insulated compartment of the swinging satellite as it came around the shoulder of Earth and into line-of-sight with the bubble of awareness now drifting, unpowered, toward the red glow of Mars. He used yoga techniques to relax, clearing his mind for the impact of the messages across ten million miles.

? (A silent question, signifying readiness to receive.)

! (A sense of excitement that didn't dim from day to day, implying that the ship was functioning perfectly, that hopes for the success of the mission were still high.)

And then:

. . . *the evil men cringed before the all-seeing wall-piercing telepathist as he stripped away the deceitful layers of hypnotic conditioning from the mind of—*

WHO'S THAT? Earthside, are you picking up a TV spectacular, for pity's sake?

. . . *the poor imprisoned girl in the ugly fortress where all her life had gone to waste, never speaking to anyone—*

Power, my God, like being hit with an iron bar! WHO ARE YOU?

. . . *weeping now with sheer relief because her wicked father was only an adopted parent and her rescuer—*

MARS SHIP CANCEL CANCEL CANCEL—speak later—that's an escapist fantasy and the way it's trending it'll be a catapathic grouping before we know where we are and —

. . . taking her from the prison into a bright world of sunshine without misery—

. . . and we can't afford to lose a mind like that! Heaven's name, can't you feel the power he has? It's unbelievable!

From the Mars ship, colored with agreement: *Where is he? Aground? Where (city) where (street)?*

Anywhere over the visible hemisphere, I guess! We've got to find him before—

And, aloud, as the communications man hammered on the wall of the insulated chamber: "Let me out of here! Fast!"

viii

Something was happening out in the real world; earlier, the city had been crisscrossed by the roar of aircraft, making a continuous din as they turned and swung back on parallel courses without ever going out of earshot, and now helicopters were droning just beyond the low gray cover of cloud. The clouds were shedding a chilly rain on the rubble-strewn site of the ruined warehouse, creating miniature lakes and rivers tinted red with brick dust. Howson wasn't interested in the outside world anyway, he told himself. Besides, it was a miserable day. Better to huddle under cover and let his imagination roam.

Curiously, though, it was becoming more difficult rather than easier to lose himself in his fantasies. Nagging ideas crawled up unbidden, to distract him. Annoyed, he con-

sidered obvious explanations: hunger, cold, irrelevant
images from the girl's mind clashing with his.

But they had eaten well during the night, and the little
fire over which they had made a mulligan stew still glowed
and made their crude shed cosy. And there was no question of the girl's mind wandering from its link with his;
she was an unbelievably passive audience, content to
obliterate everything from her awareness but the tempting
visions Howson could create.

Nonetheless the distractions continued, at the very edge
of consciousness, and were so labile that the act of turning his attention to them altered them. It might seem for
a few seconds that he was thinking: *This is childish; why
don't I go and learn to use my talents properly?* Then,
when he tried to blot out that, he was thinking: *That
way lies danger; I might forget my body and starve
while I'm day dreaming.* And the angry counter to that
—*Should I care?*—was itself countered: *Die, without
knowing the intimacy of telepathic friendship?*

He gasped and opened his eyes, sitting up with a jerk.
A stab of pain from cramp-stiffened back muscles followed the movement. Beside him, the girl whimpered her
complaint at losing contact. He ignored her, scrambled to
his feet and plunged through the sacking-screened opening
which served as their doorway.

Outside, the rain drizzled down, scarcely thick enough
to veil the surrounding buildings, but quite enough to
make it impossible to stare upward when he tried it. The
water, dirty with city smoke and dust, ran into his eyes
and made him blink helplessly. Besides, what he was
looking for was hidden behind the clouds still.

Hidden! How could *he* hide?

That last distracting concept, the one which had jolted
him to his feet, had been neither his own nor the girl's.
Behind its simple verbalization had lain layer on layer of
remembered experience, belonging to a telepathist with
full training and tremendous skill. He didn't have to have
previous knowledge to sense that. The message was self-
identifying.

So they had come for him, who could not run and had
not yet learned how to blank out his projections.

The din of the helicopters battered at his ears, the

rain stung his eyes. Without forethought, he found himself stumbling across the uneven ground; a patch of slimy mud moved under his foot, and he was sprawling in a puddle. Heedless of wet and dirt, he got up again, hearing the formless bubbling voice of the girl behind him, sensing that the hunters had located him now beyond doubt, expecting momentarily that the angular insect shapes of the helicopters would buzz through the gray overcast and close on him like vultures circling a lost explorer.

And there was one of them! Gasping, cursing, he turned, slipping and sliding and clutching whatever support he could to prevent another headlong fall. A fast vertical gale hammered the top of his head with accelerated raindrops, like birdshot, as the copter passed above him, and stayed there. The down draft formed a cage around him, its bars the needles of rain.

The girl was screaming now, as nearly as she could; the disgusting noise of her moans blended in confusion with the hammer of the copter engine.

Telepathist, why are you afraid?

The silent voice came into his head like a cold cleansing wind, islanding his consciousness in the eye of the hurricane of noise and fear. It was laden with encouragement to accept what was happening. For a moment he was too startled to resist the intrusion; this wasn't a random concept picked up by himself from a passive mind, but a deliberate projection with the force of years of mental discipline behind it. Then the second helicopter dropped into view, and he found strength in terror.

NO NO NO LEAVE ME ALONE!

The thought blasted out unaimed, and the copter directly above him reacted as though he had riddled it with gunfire. Its nose dipped, it twisted and slid across the bare ground, it jerked crazily as one of its outstretched legs crashed into the wall of the ruined warehouse, and turned over around the point of impact. On its side, it fell crunching among piled rubble, and the rotor blades snapped like dry sticks and the engine died instantly.

Unbelieving, Howson watched it crash, hardly daring to accept that he could have been responsible. Yet he knew he was: he had sensed the blinding shock in the pilot's

mind as all his reflexes were deranged. Moreover, he had
driven out the mental voice of the telepathist addressing
him, and where the link had formed between them there
was a sensation like a half-healed bruise.

In the same instant he also realized that the girl's mind
had been switched off, and when he looked, he saw she
had slumped unconscious in the mud.

Elation seized him briefly. If he could do this, he could
do anything! Let them come for him; he would drive them
back with blasts of mental resistance until they did what
he wanted and left him alone.

And then he felt the pain.

From the shattered hulk of the helicopter, it welled out
in black blinding waves, beyond all conscious control, and
was aimed at Howson by the coexistent awareness of the
sufferers that he was responsible. He gasped, thinking
his own leg was broken, his own rib cage crushed, his
own head laid open and bleeding by a sharp metal edge.
Into his startled mind the telepathist reached again.

You did that.

LEAVE ME ALONE!

And this time the surviving copter remained steady,
the telepathic link only trembled and did not break, because the fury of Howson's projection was muted by the
received pain. He started to move again, swaying, vaguely
intending to hide in the ruined warehouse, and trying to
form contradictions to answer the telepathist's accusations

*Leave me alone. I don't want to be important! When I
get involved with the world bad things happen* (confusion
of concepts radiated from this: police waiting at his
door, the helicopter pilot snatching convulsively at his
controls).

He clambered up a mound of bricks and broken lumps
of concrete, toward a wall in which half a window frame
made a gap like a single battlement. The cool projection
of the telepathist continued.

*You waste your talent on fantasy. You don't know how
to use it. That's why disaster—like a fast car you never
learn to drive!* And skillfully associated with the message,
were images that made the pile of rubble seem to be the
shell of a wrecked car, burning against the wall it had hit
head-on.

Giddy with pain, panicking because the richness of this communication was so casual and so far beyond his own untrained competence, Howson came to the top of the pile of debris and swayed in the opening of the half-window. There was a drop of twelve feet beyond, into what had been a basement level. Horrified, he thought of jumping down.

I can protect you from fear and pain. Let me.

NO NO NO LEAVE ME ALONE!

The contact wavered; the telepathist seemed to gather his strength. He "said": *All right, you deserve this for being a fool. Hold still!*

A grip like iron closed on the motor centers of Howson's brain. His hands clutched the frame of the old window, his feet found a steady purchase on its sill, and after that he could not move; the telepathist had frozen his limbs. He could not even scream his terror at discovering that this was possible.

Then images appeared.

A door giving onto an alley. Creaking open. Behind, the form of a man, skeletally thin, eyes bloodshot, cheeks sunken, dragging himself on by sheer will power. Through the door it could be seen that he had left a smeared trail in a layer of dust on the floor.

Half in, half out of the entrance, he collapsed. Time passed; a child chasing a ball down the alley found him, and went screaming to look for help.

A policeman came, made the starved man comfortable on his coat for a pillow. A doctor came with ambulance attendants. The trail in the dust was noticed, and the policeman and the doctor went into the dark passageway, tracing the man's progress.

And now a room lit through dirty panes—a pigsty of a room containing four more skeletal shapes, a woman and three men, on empty wooden crates covered with rags, incapable of thought or movement, and on their faces and hands—

Howson revolted, vomit rising in his throat, but the stern mental grip held.

On their faces, on their eyelids and in the creases of their foreheads and behind their ears and everywhere:

dust. Settled gently and inexorably because they could not move to disturb it.

That one was a telepathist, the message said. *His name was Vargas. He too preferred to lose himself in fantasies, performed to an admiring audience. He, and the audience, died.*

Howson screamed. He managed it. He forced off the grasp that held him captive, and swayed, and knew in an instant of insane terror that he had lost his balance and was tumbling. His last conscious thought was of a tree branch and a bruise that had lasted weeks without healing.

"You're going to be all right."

The words were spoken aloud, and subtly reinforced by a mental indication of confidence in the future. Howson opened his eyes to see a calm face above him. It was rather a good-looking face, in fact, and it wore a smile.

He licked his lips and tried to croak an answer, but his mind was ahead of his voice.

"Don't bother trying to talk. I'm the telepathist—I'm Danny Waldemar."

Awareness of bandages on his head and arms: a confused question.

"You're all right! We gave you prothrombin the moment we realized you were bleeding so badly. All the cuts are scabbing over." And abruptly, a switch to telepathy: *You're a miracle, do you know that? You could have died a hundred times over, from accidents!*

He hadn't done so, and therefore the point seemed irrelevant. He pursued a more important matter.

What's going to happen to me? The question was blurred with fear and vague images of human vivisection.

"Don't be afraid." Waldemar spoke aloud, slowly, with emphasis. "Nothing can be done to you that you don't understand. Nothing! From now on and forever you can always know what anyone is doing, and why!"

Of . . . course! Howson felt a sort of smile come to his twisted face, and at its reassuring appearance Waldemar chuckled and got to his feet.

Load you aboard the copter now. Get you somewhere and attend to those cuts properly.

Wait.

Waldemar checked, expressing attention.

The girl. She's deaf and dumb. I was all she had—all that mattered in her life. If you take me you've got to take her, too. It's not fair.

Surprised, Waldemar pursed his lips. There was a momentary sensation of listening, as though he had made a mental investigation and been satisfied.

"Yes, why not? It's absurd that anyone should be left like that nowadays. Her brain's uninjured, and that means she can have an artificial voice, artificial ears. . . . Why not? We'll take her with us, by all means."

Howson closed his eyes. He was fairly certain that the suggestion had been planted in his mind by Waldemar, but he didn't care. The only thing that mattered was that he was content with what had happened, and the future no longer made him terrified.

A mental chuckle came to him from Waldemar, and then he slept.

Book Two   Agitat

*H*owson sat staring dully out over Ulan Bator, thinking how much its condition resembled his own. He
could sense its collective mood; for the rest of his
life he would be unendingly subject to a kind of emotional
weather, the sum of the individual minds surrounding
him.

The city had been a rather dowdy, provincial-feeling
one, even though it was the capital of a country. The
changing pattern of the world—transport, commerce, communications—had hurried it into modern times; now it was
a place of fine white towers and broad avenues, and
travelers of all kinds came. Amid the turmoil of change,
old people could do no more than wonder what had hit
them, and long without enthusiasm for the simpler past.

So, too, he had been overtaken by a change he didn't
want, and believed he would accept only if other changes
were found to be possible—changes he did desire.

It wasn't that they had not been kind to him. They had
gone to a great deal of trouble. Apart from the immensely
thorough medical examinations their specialists had given
him—and this hospital at Ulan Bator was the main
therapy center for WHO in all Asia, with staff commensu-
rate—there were such minor luxuries as this chair in
which he sat. It was subtly designed to accommodate him,
Gerald Howson; it was smaller than usual, and the padding
matched his deformities. The bed was designed for him,
too, and the equipment in the adjacent bathroom, and
everything.

But he didn't want that. It was the same as being

helped onto a crowded bus: a hateful reminder of his handicap.

There came a tapping at the door. Automatically he turned his attention to the visitor—no, visitors. So far he had accepted almost no formal training in the use of his talent, but there were trained telepathists on the permanent staff of the hospital, and merely being close to them had increased his control and sensitivity. He couldn't help admiring them—who could? But so far he had learned nothing about them which reconciled him to being what they were not: a runt, and deformed into the bargain.

He said, both aloud and telepathically, in a tone hinged with weariness, "All right, come in."

Pandit Singh was the first to enter. A burly man running to fat, with a neatly combed beard and sharp bright eyes, he was the head of therapy A—responsible, in other words, for all neurological and psychological treatment undertaken at the hospital. People, including Howson, liked him; Howson had been impressed by the fact that his sympathy was always colored by determination to *do* something if possible. Too many people's pity was soured by relief that they at least were physically whole.

Along with him had come Danny Waldemar and one of the staff neurologists, a woman named Christine Bakwa, whom Howson had met previously in one of the many examination rooms he had been taken to. She wasn't good at disciplining her verbalized thoughts, the most easily accessible to a casual telepathic "glance," and even before she entered the room Howson had learned from her most of what Singh had to say.

Nonetheless, he made a curt gesture indicating that they should sit down, and turned his own chair on its smoothly operating casters to face Singh.

"Morning, Gerry," Singh said. "I hear your girl friend was around to see you. How is she? I meant to have a word with her, but I was too busy."

"She's getting on well," Howson said. She was; she was becoming used to the impulses given off by the trembler coils deft surgeons had inserted in her ears, and the bio-activated plastic vocal cords that had replaced her own. There was promise that she would stumble into possession of a musical, if hesitant, speaking voice once she had completed training. Howson slapped down envy at her childish joy, and added the question to which he already sensed the answer.

"And how about me?"

Singh looked at him steadily. He said, "You know I have bad news for you. I couldn't conceivably hide the fact."

"Spell it out," Howson said stubbornly.

"Very well." Singh sighed. He gestured to Christine Bakwa, and she gave him a folder of papers from a portfolio she was carrying. Selecting the topmost enclosure, he continued, "To begin with, Gerry, there's the question of your grandfather—your mother's father."

"He died long before I was born," Howson muttered.

"That's right. Were you ever told why he died so young?"

Howson shook his head. "I guess I knew my mother didn't like talking about it, so I never pushed the point to an answer."

"Well, she must have known. He was what they call a hemophiliac—in other words, a bleeder, whose normal supply of thrombic enzyme was absent. He ought never to have had children. But he did, and through your mother you inherited the condition."

"I told you this," Danny Waldemar put in. "When we were taking you aboard the helicopter—remember? I told you we'd given you prothrombin, which is an artificial clotting agent. Your scratches and bruises have always taken a long time to heal, haven't they? A serious hemorrhage—a nosebleed, say—would have put you in the hospital for a month, and quite possibly would have killed you. You're lucky to be alive."

Am I? Howson kept the counter on the telepathic level, but it was so bitter Waldemar flinched visibly.

Aloud, Howson objected, "So what? Prothrombin works on me: the cuts I got when you picked me up healed fast enough once the scabs had formed."

Singh exchanged a glance with his companion. Before he could speak again, Howson had caught on to what was in the big Indian's mind.

"No?" he whispered.

"No. I'm sorry, Gerry. Those cuts in fact healed at barely half the rate you'd expect in a healthy person. And anything much more serious than a cut—say a broken bone—will probably never heal at all. Yet paradoxically this is what has made you the most promising novice telepathist to come to our notice since Ilse Kronstadt. Let me make that clear."

He held up the paper from the file so that Howson could see it. It was a large black-and-white schematic representation of a human brain. At the base of the cortex, a small red arrow had been inked in.

"You've probably picked up most of what I have to tell you," he said. "As Danny pointed out when you first met, you need never again fail to understand what's being done to you and why. But I'll go over it, if you don't mind; not being a telepathist myself, I organize words better than unverbalized concepts."

Howson nodded, staring with aching misery at the drawing.

"Information is stored in the brain rather casually," Singh went on. "There's so much spare capacity, you see. But there are certain areas where particular data are normally concentrated, and what we call 'body image'—a sort of reference standard of the condition of the body—is kept where that arrow's marked. A great deal of the data required for healing is right down on the cellular level, naturally, but in your case that mechanism's faulty—witness your hemophilia. One could get around that with the aid of artificial stimulation of your body-image center, but for this paradox I mentioned."

He changed the drawing for another, showing the brain from below, also bearing a red arrow.

"Now, here's a typical average brain—like mine or Christine's. The red arrow points to a group of cells called the organ of Funck. It's so small its very existence was overlooked until the first telepathists were discovered. In my brain, for instance, it consists of about a hundred cells, not much different from their neighbors. You'll note its location."

Again he extracted a fresh item from the folder. This one was a large X-ray transparency, the whitish outline of a skull with jaw and neck vertebrae.

"You'll remember we took X rays of your head, Gerry, after giving you a radio-opaque substance which selectively . . . ah . . . 'stains' cells in the organ of Funck. Take a look at the result."

Howson gazed numbly at the picture.

"That whitish mass at the base of the brain," Singh said. "It's your organ of Funck. It's the largest, by almost twenty per cent, that I've ever seen. Potentially you have the most powerful telepathic faculty in the world, because that's the organ which resonates with impulses in other nervous systems. You are capable of coping with an amount of information that staggers the mind."

"And it's made me a cripple," Howson said.

"Yes." Slowly Singh put the picture away. "Yes, Gerry. It's taken over the space normally occupied by body image, and as a result we can do nothing to mend your body. Any operation big enough to help you would also be big enough to kill you."

"Well, Danny?" said Singh when they had returned to his office. The telepathist, whose specialty was the discovery and training of new members of his kind, slowly shook his head.

"He has no reason to cooperate," he said. "My God, do you blame him? Think about his plight! His face, every time he looks in the mirror—like an idiot child about to vomit! What compensation is it after twenty years of *that* to become a telepathist? I've picked out things from his mind . . ." He paused, swallowing hard.

"Consider! He was first overheard from orbit, by a space communicator, so potentially his 'voice' is the loudest in history. But his real voice has never broken—he has this silly castrato pipe! He never lost his milk teeth, for God's sake; just as well, in view of his hemophilia, but think what that did to his psyche. It takes him three months to grow enough hair to visit the barber. He's never even begun to have a beard. As to sexuality, he's acquired superficial attitudes and never experienced the emotions; what that'll do to him the first time he contacts someone with a bad sexual problem, God knows."

"Can we tackle that?" Singh suggested.

"Out of the question!" Waldemar snapped. "You can't

seriously want to make his condition worse—and believe me, you would, if you made him sexually competent with hormones and left him in this malformed body. Mark you, I'm not sure you'd succeed; his body image is so far from normal, I daren't guess whether he can respond to hormones or not."

"What I was thinking was—" put in Christine Bakwa, and broke off. Waldemar glanced at her.

"You were wondering if I could take his mind apart and put it together again, hm? To clear out this terrible jealousy he's conceived for his girl friend?"

"Yes, I was." The neurologist made a vague gesture. "I see why he's so resentful; I mean, fitting her up with speech and hearing was so easy he must subconsciously disbelieve that helping him is impossible, and the very fact that he made it a condition of coming with you suggests that he's got high empathy."

"Granted," Waldemar agreed. "Only . . . he's powerful."

"I thought you managed to control him when you first located him."

"Briefly. I'd never have got in at all but that he was suffering terribly from the knowledge that he'd caused the pain of the man in the copter that crashed. And he broke my hold eventually. No, in cold blood he could resist any attempt made to interfere with his mind, and I'm not sure the telepathist who attempted it would retain his sanity."

There was a hollow silence. It was broken by a soft buzz from a phone on Singh's desk. Heavily he moved to depress the attention switch.

"Yes?"

"Mr. Hemmikaini is here for you, Dr. Singh," a voice reported.

"Oh! Oh, very well. Send him up." Singh let go the switch and glanced at his companions. "That's one of the Special Assistants to the UN Secretary General coming in. I guess I have to worry about what he wants rather than spending all my time thinking of Howson. But with the potential Howson represents . . ."

Getting to his feet, Waldemar finished the sentence for him. "One could wish," he muttered, "that the rest of the damned world would stop nagging at us for a few days and let us get through the wall of his resentment! Somebody ought to work it out sometime—whether we telepathists have caused more bother than we've saved."

He gave Singh a crooked grin and went out.

x

*H*emmikaini was a large, round-faced man with fair hair cut extremely short, and very pink skin. He looked like what he was—a successful and dedicated executive. It was only the nature of his duties that was unusual.

After giving Singh a plump-fingered hand and setting his black portfolio on the corner of the desk, he dropped into a chair and leaned back.

"Well, you know why I'm here, Dr. Singh. You also know that time is running short, so I'll waste none of it on fiddling courtesies. We have a problem. We have computer solutions to indicate that we need someone with talents of the order possessed by Ilse Kronstadt. Ergo, we need her—she's unique. Yet our request for the release of her services, made to the director in chief here,-was countered by the suggestion that somebody should come and talk to you. Why?"

Singh placed his elbows on the desk, looked down at his hands, and meticulously put the tips of the fingers together. Without raising his head, he said, "In effect, what you want to know is what Ilse Kronstadt can possibly be doing here that we regard as more important than a UN pacification operation."

Hemmikaini blinked. After a pause he nodded. "Since you put it so bluntly, I'll agree to that."

Singh made a musing sound. He said, "It's Southern Africa again, I suppose?"

"'A fair guess, if you've been reading newspapers. But I'll make one correction." Hemmikaini leaned forward impressively. "It's not just 'Southern Africa *again*,' in that tone of voice! Ever since the Black Trek, when half the South African labor force walked out of the country, it's been a thorn in our flesh—was previously, for pity's sake! We've gone back and back to tidy up after each successive burst of terrorism and violence, and we thought we'd finally solved the problem. We haven't . . . quite. But this time we want to do what we've been hoping to do ever since we first had telepathists to help us."

"You want to stop it before it happens," Singh murmured.

"Correct. We have nearly enough data now. Makerakera has been there for three months, with all the staff we can spare. But the deadline is too close. We need Ilse Kronstadt, to beat it."

Singh got up from the desk abruptly and strode to the window. Thumbing the switch to "full transparency," he gazed out over Ulan Bator. His back to Hemmikaini, he said, "You can't have her, I'm afraid."

"What?" Hemmikaini bridled. "Now look here, Dr. Singh—!" He checked, realizing the brusqueness of his tone, and went on more politely, "Is that Dr. Kronstadt's answer?"

"I have no idea. The request hasn't even been put to her."

"Then what in hell's name do you mean?" Hemmikaini made no attempt to remain calm this time.

"You must presumably have wondered," Singh said, "why Ilse left the UN Pacification Agency, where she virtually pioneered the techniques of nonviolent control that have subsequently become standard practice."

"Yes, of course I have," Hemmikaini snapped.

"And?"

"Well . . . well, I guess I assumed she wanted a change. She worked herself to exhaustion often enough, for pity's sake!"

"Further than exhaustion, Mr. Hemmikaini." Singh turned now, and the light from the window caught the graying tips of his hair and beard. "Ilse Kronstadt is the next best thing to a dead woman."

Hemmikaini's bright-pink lips parted. No sound emerged.

"Customarily," Singh went on inexorably, "someone as indispensable as Ilse is watched by doctors, psychologists, a horde of experts. There was a succession of crises a few years ago—India, Indonesia, Portugal, Latvia, Guiana, in a stream—and these precautions were temporarily let slide. Afterward we discovered a malignant tumor in Ilse's brain. If we'd caught it early enough, we could have extirpated it microsurgically; a little later, and we could have used ultrasound or focused electron beams. As it happened, there is now no way of removing it short of major surgery from *below* the cortex."

"Oh, my God," said Hemmikaini. He wasn't looking at Singh. Probably he couldn't. "You mean you'd have to cut through her telepathic organ to get to it."

"Precisely."

"Does she know?"

"Have *you* ever tried to keep a secret from a telepathist? Only another telepathist can manage it, and in Ilse's case I'm not sure anyone else has been born who could keep her out if she was really determined. She's capable of handling the total personality of another human being, you know—or the 'I-now' awareness of about a dozen simultaneously."

Singh turned his hand over in the air as though spilling a pile of dust from the palm. "You can't have her, Mr. Hemmikaini. So long as she's here, we can keep her alive and husband her energy for her. She's not an invalid, exactly—she lives a life similar to anyone else's on the staff—but she only undertakes one type of work, and that seldom."

"Because of the strain?"

"Naturally."

Hemmikaini licked his lips. "What work does she do, then?"

"Do you know what a catapathic grouping is?" Singh asked. On the answering headshake, he amplified. "It's a bastard word, coined from 'catalepsy' and 'telepathic,' of course. Every now and again a telepathist turns out to be an inadequate personality. Maybe he tackles a job too big for him. Maybe he just can't face the responsibilities that go with his talent. Or maybe he finds the world generally insupportable." He thought briefly of Howson, crippled, undersized, and hurried on.

"He prefers to retreat into fugue and make a fantasy world which is more tolerable. Well, everyone does that occasionally. A telepathist, though, can do it on the grand scale. He can provide himself with an audience—as many as eight people, if he's powerful—and take them into fugue with him. We call them 'reflective personalities'; they mirror and feed the telepathist's ego.

"When that happens, they forget not just the world but even their bodies. They don't feel hunger or thirst or pain. And as you'd expect, they don't want to wake up."

"Do they *never* wake up?" Hammikaini demanded.

"Oh, eventually. But you see, not feeling hunger and thirst doesn't mean they don't exist. After five to seven days there is irreversible damage to the brain, and what does finally wake them is the sinking of the telepathist's power below the level at which he can maintain the complex linkage. And by then, they're past hope."

"What's this got to do with Ilse Kronstadt?"

"Even an inadequate telepathist is precious," Singh said. "There is one chance to save a catapathic grouping, if it's found in time. You have to break into the fantasy world and make it even less tolerable than reality. And Ilse is the one person alive who can consistently succeed. So you see, Mr. Hemmikaini"—he permitted himself a grim smile—"I do have an answer to your question: what can possibly be more important as a job for Ilse than a major UN pacification assignment? She's saved almost two dozen telepathists for the future; collectively, they've done far more than she could even as a well woman."

Hemmikaini was silent for a while. At length he asked, "How long has she got to live?"

"She might die of exhaustion during her next therapeutic session. She might live five years. It's a guess."

Again, silence. Then the UN man pulled himself together and rose. "Thank you for the explanation, Dr. Singh," he muttered. "We'll just have to make do with our second best, I suppose."

It was later in the day that, moved by an unaccountable

impulse, Singh went up to the apartment in the west wing of the hospital where Ilse Kronstadt lived. He found her sitting at a typewriter, her fine-boned hands flying over the keys like hummingbirds, the air full of the soft hum of the motor.

"Come in, Pan," she invited. "One moment and I'll be with you."

Singh complied, closing the door. He could not help looking at her, thinking of the way she had changed since he first knew her. The fair hair had gone absolutely white; the strong face was networked with wrinkles, and the healthy tan of her skin was turning to a waxen pallor.

"Yes, Pan, I know," she said gently. She stripped the paper from the machine and turned to face him. "It makes me frightened sometimes. . . . That's why I'm exorcising it, of course."

"What do you mean?" Singh muttered.

"I've decided to write my autobiography," she answered. A mischievous grin crossed her face. "A certain best seller, they tell me! Oh, sit down, Pan! No need to be ceremonious with me, is there? Especially since I sent for you."

Surprise died the instant it took shape in Singh's mind. He chuckled and moved to a chair. Ilse Kronstadt leaned her elbow on the back of her own chair and cupped her sharp chin in her palm.

"You're worried, Pan," she said in an abrupt reversion to a serious tone. "It's been making the place gloomy for days. Most of it's because of this novice Danny picked up—poor guy!—but this morning I noticed I'd got fouled up in it, so I thought I'd have a chat. I hope you appreciate my waiting till you weren't engaged."

"Did you really need to send for me, Ilse?" Singh spoke the words because he knew the thought had emerged too forcibly into consciousness to disguise it anyhow.

"Yes, Pan." The words dropped like stones. "It's getting worse. I need to economize on the use of my telepathy now; I tire quickly, and I get confused. It makes me feel very old."

There was silence. Not looking at him, she went on at last, "You know, I'd have liked to marry, have children. . . . I think I'd have tried it, in spite of everything, if I hadn't seen from the inside what hell it is to be a non-telepathist child of telepathists. Remember Nola Grüning?"

"I do," Singh muttered. Nola Grüning had married—a telepathist, naturally; it was the only sane course—and had a child which didn't inherit. And she had wound up in a catapathic grouping of children, her fantasies bright nursery images, from which Ilse had had to detach the reflective personalities one by one, leaving Nola hopelessly insane.

"So!" Ilse said with forced brightness. "So the autobiography. I can leave words behind, at least. Now tell me what it was that brought me into the pattern of your worry."

Singh didn't trouble to speak; he merely marshaled the facts in his mind for her to inspect.

She sighed. "You're right, of course, Pan. I couldn't face a situation that complex—not any more. It would break me into little pieces. It's the frustration, you see. You tackle the big problem, and it leaves unsolved scores, maybe thousands of small problems, and every single one hurts. . . . I used to be able to resign myself. I—I've been forced now to resign period."

She moved as though shrugging off a bad dream. "Still, people have gone blind, people have gone crazy, since the dawn of history. I'm still human, after all! Is Danny getting anywhere with his novice, by the way?"

"Not yet. That's why I've been radiating worry, of course."

"What a damned shame! Sometimes I think I was unbelievably lucky in spite of everything, Pan. At least I had intelligent parents, a healthy childhood, first-rate education. . . . Assuming the late appearance of the gift—never before seventeen, most often at twenty or over—is a kind of natural insurance against it destroying an immature personality, I reckon I was just about as well equipped as I could have been. But he's a real mess, isn't he? Orphaned, crippled, hemophiliac . . ."

"Have you any ideas that would help Danny?" Singh ventured.

"You're late, Pan!" She gave a harsh laugh. "Danny asked me a week ago if I could help."

"And can you?"

Her face went blank, as if a light behind it had been turned off. Stonily she said, "I daren't, Pan. I've touched the fringes of his mind. I sheered off. In the old days I might have risked it—I'd have banked on my experience outweighing the naked power he possesses. I could have insured against him panicking. I'm too old to cope with him now, Pan—and too sick."

"What's going to become of him, then? Are we likely to lose him?" Singh spoke thickly.

"I can't reach deep enough into his personality to tell you. Obviously, he has empathy waiting to be tapped; if it is, he'll be my successor. You realize that, I hope? If it isn't, he may hate himself into insanity. What we could do to tip the balance I just don't *know*, Pan! I tell you, I daren't look so far into his mind!"

xi

There came a time not long afterward when they started to leave Howson alone, and—as he was honest enough to admit when he took a firm grip on himself—that too became a source of resentment. The way he analyzed his feelings, his desire to be treated as important was still active in his subconscious; his mood of stubborn resistance to Singh's pleading, Waldemar's telepathic persuasion, was satisfying in a back-to-front fashion because it was a means of ensuring the continuation of their interest. Once he had yielded and begun to cooperate, most of his training would be done by himself. Another telepathist could only guide him away from blind alleys. Each was unique, and each had to teach himself.

Of course, that was only half of it. The other half looked at him out of the mirror.

So much was easy to understand. Other things puzzled him a little. The rather gingerly way in which Waldemar approached a contact with him was mystifying for a long while after his arrival in Ulan Bator; one day, however, Waldemar's control over the explanation slipped, and the reason emerged into plain view. He was afraid that Howson might become insane, and the possibility of an insane telepathist with Howson's power was bleakly fearful.

More appalling still was the discovery Howson made after the idea had germinated in his own mind: the idea of escape into madness had a horrid fascination, offering a chance to exercise unbridled power without the restraint imposed by causing suffering which he would in turn experience—as he had experienced the pain of the men in the crashed helicopter.

Before the incident which distracted everybody's attention from him, he had allowed himself to be shown over the hospital, and had found it sufficiently interesting to want to limp down the corridors by himself occasionally, unchallenged by the staff, who had received instructions from Singh never to interfere wth him. He had felt recurrent pangs of envy, though, each time he considered a patient on the way to recovery, whether from a mental or a physical illness, and now he preferred to sit brooding in his room, letting his mind rove. That he could not resist; as he had learned when the gift first made its appearance, there was no way to close it off as simple as shutting one's eyes.

When he opened up to maximum sensitivity, the hospital, and the city beyond, became a chaos of nonsense. He was developing his powers of selection, though, and proving for himself what he found he had subconsciously assumed: accuracy was a function not so much of range as of extraneous mental "noise," and careful concentration would enable him to pick a single mind out of thousands in the same way one can follow a single speaker amid the hubbub of a lively party.

Some personalities were very easy to pick out; they bloomed like fireballs against a black sky. The staff telepathists were naturally the easiest of all, but he was reluctant to make contact with them; he sensed a basic friendliness when he did so, yet it was discolored because to them it seemed so obvious that any telepathist would

want the gift he had received, and they were puzzled
and upset by Howson's depression.

In any case, all but one of them were preoccupied
with their work. The exception was the possessor of a mind
that lighted the whole of one wing of the hospital with an
invisible radiance so bright that it shielded the personality
behind it. He had probed around the fringes of that
radiance, and sensed an aura of confident power that
gave him pause; then, unexpectedly, there had been a disturbance in the personality, and the aura darkened and
almost faded away. If one could imagine a star overcome
by weariness, one might comprehend what had happened.
Howson found it beyond him; he preferred to turn his
attention elsewhere.

He had asked whose this remarkable mind was,
naturally, and the answer—that it was the half-legendary
Ilse Kronstadt, on whom had been based a character in
the movie he had watched along with the man in brown—
made him even less inclined to pester her.

There were also the non-telepathists who stood out.
Singh was the most striking. He had a mind as clear as
standing water, into which one might plunge indefinitely
without fathoming the limits of his compassion. Again,
though, Howson preferred not to dip into Singh's awareness. Too much of it was concerned with his own plight,
and the patent impossibility of healing his deformity.

He chose rather to touch the minds that were more
ordinary—staff and patients. At first he moved with utmost
caution; then as he grew surer of his skill he grew bolder
also, and spent long hours in contemplation that appealed
to him the same way as movies and TV had formerly done.
This was so much richer that the TV set standing in a
corner of his room was not turned on after the first week of
his stay.

The hospital held patients and staff of more than fifty
nationalities. Their languages, customs, hopes and fears
were endlessly fascinating to him, and it was only when he
came back to reality, drunk with the delight of shared experience, after a voyage through a dozen minds, that he
found himself seriously inclined to fall in with the wishes of
Singh and Waldemar.

Yet he still hung back. There was one group of patients

in the hospital whose minds he could not fail to be aware of, and who were sometimes responsible for his waking in the middle of the night, sweat-drenched, a victim of nameless terrors. They were the insane, lost in their private universes of illogic, and of course it was among them that the work of the staff telepathists lay.

Once, and only once, he "watched" a telepathic psychiatrist brace himself for a therapeutic session. The patient was a paranoid with an obsessive sexual jealousy, and the telepathist was attempting to locate the root experiences behind it. It was too big a job to be completed by telepathy, of course; once the experiences had been identified, there would be hypnosis, drug-abreaction and probably a regression in coma to bring the man to terms with his past. At the moment, though, his brain was a hell of irrational torments, and the telepathist had to pick his way through them like a man braving a jungle crammed with monsters.

Howson did not stay with the psychiatrist past that point. But he was more afraid than ever afterward.

And then the crisis broke, and Howson, uncooperative, was left on one side while frantic attempts were made at rescue.

His picture of what was really going on remained for a long time rather confused. He hadn't bothered to look at a newspaper or switch on a TV news bulletin for weeks now; if he had done so he would have learned immediately that Hemmikaini's "second best" hadn't been good enough, and as a result the crisis in Southern Africa had turned into a dirty, bloody, tangled mess.

While Makerakera, the expert on aggression, sweated frantically to weld together a scratch team of whoever could be spared to join him—Choong from Hong Kong, Jenny Pender from Indiana, Stanislaus Danquah from Accra, and some trainees—the little Greek Pericles Phranakis turned his back on the catastrophe and went away down a path of his own, to a land where success had crowned his efforts with a wreath of bay.

At Salisbury, Nairobi, Johannesburg, the troops came down from the sky; after them, the mobile hospitals, the transport copters, the cans and sacks and bales of basic food; after them, the jurists and the politicians (what do you do with a man in jail on a murder charge when the organs of the arraigning government collapse?). A great hollow silence succeeded the tumult, and it was broken by the sound of children crying.

Meantime, a Mach Five stratoplane carried the shell of Pericles Phranakis to Ulan Bator, and the computers were proved right: it would take Ilse Kronstadt to cope with the crisis, and if she couldn't go to it, it would come to her.

Howson caught stray images from the fantasy Phranakis was enjoying, and shuddered. He was reminded strongly of his own daydreams, which—according to Danny Waldemar, at least—might finally have tempted him to enter a catapathic grouping with the deaf-and-dumb girl. Thinking of the first such, he remembered the dust on Vargas' eyes, and almost moaned aloud.

A curious sense of isolation had resulted from the diversion of everyone's thoughts to Phranakis, and in a panic because he was experiencing loneliness—worse by contrast with the month-long flow of concern about him that he had been basking in—he hastened to involve himself with the problems occupying the outstanding minds near him.

He did not immediately venture to intrude on the privacy of Ilse Kronstadt herself, but he sensed her anxiety like a bad odor. Dimly he grasped the fact that even if Phranakis had failed, he was still regarded as the nearest competitor she had in her original specialty, the elimination of aggression; facing the task of breaking open his fantasy, she quailed.

Embarrassed, he switched his attention elsewhere, and found Phranakis forming a paranoid obsession in the forefront of the staff's collective mind. Like a flight of crows following a plowman, people who knew him were coming in, and the voices of the dead on paper and on record and on film spoke guidance to Ilse Kronstadt. When he was five years old, he did such-and-so; with his first girl, he liked to do this; during his training in telepathy, he had difficulty with that.

As a sculptor might take odds and ends of scrap metal and fuse them into a work of art, Ilse Kronstadt now selected from these data and created a mental image of Phranakis. Howson was fascinated; he was so absorbed that he never realized when he trespassed on her awareness for the first time. Either he did not notice that he was "watching" her, or she was too preoccupied to care. He thought the latter, and felt a stab of guilt at his unwillingness to exploit his own talent as she was exploiting hers.

Sitting still as stone in the special chair more comfortable than any he had ever used before, he absorbed the self-disciplining methods by which she built up her sagging confidence. There were glimpses of past successes, which had seemed equally daunting yet which ended in triumph; there were concepts of self-esteem, conceit almost, deliberately fostered to strengthen her determination.

Howson followed all this with jaw-cramping concentration. Even so, when he let his mind wander toward Phranakis, he was shaken. How could anyone—even the unprecedented Dr. Kronstadt—disturb the armored fantasy around the man's ego now?

He forgot he was Gerald Howson. He forgot he was a cripple, a runt, a bleeder, an orphan. He remembered only that he was a telepathist, able to snatch facts from any mind he chose if the owner gave permission, and with desperate eagerness filled out his knowledge of what had led to this impasse.

Phranakis: this was how he felt to himself before he went into fugue; this was the face he saw daily in his mirror; this was the mother he remembered, the father, the brothers and sisters; this was the road that took him to Athens and the disappointments of early manhood, this was the room where he was first shocked into knowledge of his real identity. . . .

Southern Africa: this was the ulcer festering below the slick modern surface; this was the hatred of dark against light skin and this was the greed that burst into violence . . . He visualized the huge Polynesian, Makerekera, walking a sunny street and absorbing hate like a camera; he was one of the rare receptive telepathists with no projective "voice," like the therapy watchdogs and lay analysts Howson had met here at the hospital. He knew images of long corridors, rooms where solemn men met to plan this first attempt to give meaning to the ancient platitude about the best time to stop a war. He sensed the reaction of Phranakis when he realized his work had failed: he saw it as nemesis, the reward of hubris, the illimitable conceit which offended the gods of his ancestors.

And he looked also into the minds and lives of those whom Phranakis had taken with him. Taken: that was the really unique aspect of this case, and the one which frightened Ilse Kronstadt worst.

For such was Phranakis' power that he had not had to wait on the willingness of the reflective personalities in his catapathic grouping. He had simply taken them over—four of his closest non-telepathic associates—and dragged them down with him into his unreal universe.

As awed and fascinated as a rabbit facing a snake, Howson traced the course of events around him. Far below, where the specialists and the high politicians and the families and friends were gathered, they were bringing Phranakis to the room where Ilse Kronstadt waited to do him battle. The hospital seemed to draw in on itself, to tauten till it sang apprehension like a fiddle string. Howson tautened with it, lost to the world, and scarcely dared to breathe.

xii

Down the streets of his brain a procession moved. As youths and maidens, garlanded with flowers, danced in his honor, the grave elders gathered at the shrine of Pallas Athene. There they made ready the wreath of bay with which to crown the champion. For all their boasts and cunning, the barbarians had gone down to defeat. The city was safe; civilization and freedom survived, while far away a tyrant cursed and ordered the execution of his generals.

There was a city, certainly. There were, in a sense, elders gathered to the presence of their champion. But Aesculapius was closer to their minds than Athene, and the crown they had prepared for his head was a light metal frame trailing leads to a complex encephalograph. There was no tyrant, apart from the demon of hate, but there were definitely barbarians, although they had passed for civilized until they were broken and demoralized. They had conquered Pericles Phranakis, and were still defying the forces sent against them. He had refused to face that knowledge, and now he had forgotten.

His swarthy face contented, he lay in what was basically a bed, but could become an extension of his body if required. Apart from the instruments monitoring every physical response—heartbeat, respiration, brain rhythms, blood pressure and a dozen more—there were elaborate prosthetics attached to him. At present he was being fed artificially, while the other devices remained inert. Should the shock of recovery prove as violent as the shock of collapse, he might relinquish all attempts to live. Then the heart masseur, the oxygenator, the artificial kidney would fight against vagal inhibition and maintain life in his body until he had painfully accepted the frustration of his planned escape from the world.

Nearby Ilse Kronstadt had composed herself amid a similar array of instruments. In a chair at her side was a young man with a pale, anxious face—a recently qualified receptive telepathist serving as her therapy watchdog. Once she had entered Phranakis' self-glorifying world, she would be unable to communicate verbally with the nervous doctors supervising the process. By turns around the clock this young man and three others would "listen" to her struggles, and report anything the doctors needed to know.

One by one the technicians, the specialists, the telepathist nodded to Singh, who stood at the foot of Ilse Kronstadt's bed remembering her past triumphs and trying not to pay too much attention to the mass of cancerous tissue spreading beneath her brain. She looked very small and old lying among the machinery of the bed, and although she had not told him directly, he knew she was afraid.

"We're ready, Ilse," he said in the levelest tone he could manage.

Without opening her eyes, she answered, "Me, too. You can keep quiet now."

Then, with no further warning, she let herself go. How it could be perceived, Singh had never been able to work out, but it was unmistakable: one second, she was conscious and aware of her body; the next, it was a shell, and *she* was in another universe.

He kept his aching eyes on the pale face of the watchdog, and was dismayed after only a couple of minutes to see a shock of surprise reflected there. In the same instant Ilse stirred.

"Strong . . ." she said in a faraway voice

The alarmed audience oozed tension almost tangibly. She licked her lips and went on, "I have the picture of his fantasy now. He's the great hero, defender of Athens, darling of the gods and idol of the people. . . . I can't break in, Pan! Not without making myself so obvious he'll summon all his will to resist."

"Take your time," Singh said reassuringly. "There's bound to be a chance to form a covering role in the fantasy. It may take time to develop, but it'll come."

"I know." The voice was faint, almost ghostly. Singh wondered how much of it he was actually hearing, how much experiencing telepathically. The bloodless lips scarcely moved. "He has fabulous control, Pan. The schizoid secondaries are unbelievably contrasted. And he's got them from the reflectives as well as from himself."

Singh bit his lip. Only superb powers of self-deception could create the schizoid secondary personalities—individuals acting their part in the drama whose thoughts and reactions were only observable, not controllable, by the telepathist's ego. Without seeming to pause, however, he uttered new comfort.

"That ought to make it easier, surely! He won't be surprised at the appearance of an intruder."

"He hasn't left *room* for intruders!" The objection was a shrill cry. "It's like a flower unfolding—it's complete and all it has to do is spread out and be perfect!"

No matter how desperately he wanted to, Singh could find no reassuring counter to that. A fantasy so elaborate

must have been Phranakis' companion for years, nurtured
in his subconscious, polished and perfected until he could
unreel it like a movie film, without any of the hesitations
or doubts which would afford an entry for the therapist,
disguised as a mere mental pawn.

Thickly he said, "Well, have patience, Ilse. When the
situation looks hopeful, we'll disturb his brain rhythms
and let you in."

No answer. Why should there be? Other, lesser ther-
apists had resorted to such crude devices; Ilse Kronstadt
had never needed to. Already, even before the job was
under way, there was a sour smell of defeat in the room.

Alice Through the Looking Glass: a path that always
turned back on itself, no matter how you struggled to
reach your goal.

A concept from relativity: the twisting of space itself.

An image from a science-fiction movie: a barrier of
force glowing blue with brush discharges.

A fragment of legend: a wall of magic fire enclosing the
place where an enchanted maiden slept away the
centuries.

So frightened by the mystery of what was happening
that he could not tear himself away from it, Howson
snatched these and other mental pictures from the minds
of those engaged in the attempt to cure Phranakis. They
were clues, no more: they were the personal labels that
had been hung on catapathic grouping by people who
found unlabeled concepts intolerable. Previously he had
accepted Waldemar's explanation. He hadn't thought that
the reality would be so far beyond preconception, the sun
beside the moon, the continent beside the map.

He had probed the minds of conscious telepathists.
There he had found the familiar world mirrored: law
ruled the passage of event, solid was solid, the senses
murmured their news of the body's condition. But Phranakis had closed and locked every door to the ordinary
world, and although there were windows—of one-way
glass facing inward, so to say—what went on behind them
was insane.

Knowing it, Howson wished with all his might for the
will to resist such temptation. He saw his own fantasies

paralleled in Phranakis'—the hero concepts, the organization of everything around his whim, so that nothing disturbed, nothing upset, nothing offended the all-wise master. Here the human will to power, checked in conscious telepathists by the deterrent of other people suffering, could find ghastly outlet. Already the sado-masochistic impulses Phranakis had so long detested were creeping from shadow and coloring the fantasy.

They were casting down captives from the Acropolis, that the city's savior might the more enjoy his triumph to the music of their screams—

Abruptly the smooth course of the action was shattered. It was like an earthquake; buildings shivered, people wavered, the sky darkened. It lasted only a moment, but the impact was staggering. Howson's contact was broken, and it was several minutes before he could resume it.

"She's in," the therapy watchdog reported, his face drawn by the strain into an inhuman mask. "A captive condemned to death. Trying to get the attention of the hero-ego."

Singh nodded thoughtfully. "That figures. Fits the data we have on his sexual preferences. Any idea what the long-term plan is?"

"Fixed for a short distance," the watchdog said. "Idea is: lure him to a sexual situation, rely on failing control to establish dominance. . . . Three main sequences envisaged—want them?"

"If nothing more interesting is developing."

"No." The watchdog had to pause and swallow hard. "The captives are still being thrown off the rock. Well, either she'll establish a quasi-real knife—under cover of a banquet, maybe—and castrate him publicly, or she'll get him into a drunken stupor and establish a fire in the temple, which is why she wanted the material on the destruction of the Parthenon, or she'll start picking off the reflectives and stage a slave revolt."

Singh closed his eyes. After all his years of work as a doctor, he was still capable of being sickened at the cold-bloodedness of some of his and his colleagues' methods. What the public castration would do to Phranakis, he dared not think—but it figured. If anything could blast him out of his fugue, that would. All the material on his sexual life pointed to the need to reassure himself about his masculinity. The real world had never threatened him with anything so horrible as what Ilse was preparing.

Howson was following developments better now. He had discovered the reason for the "earthquake"—some sort of electrical impulse had been applied to Phranakis' organ of Funck, to make an opening for Ilse Kronstadt. Now it was much easier to eavesdrop; she made a link with normal consciousness. With fascinated disgust he came to comprehend her plans, and had to force himself to remember that unless something brutal jarred him out of his pleasant dream, Phranakis was as good as dead, and along with him four valuable, hard-working non-telepathists whose precious individuality he had trampled on. In a sense he deserved what was coming. But . . . could *anyone* really deserve it?

"She's getting very tired," the watchdog whispered, as though Ilse could overhear him. That was absurd: nothing could reach her now except the full violence of another telepathist. All her energy had been transmuted to will power as she altered, added to and undermined the pattern of Phranakis' fantasy.

"Is the crisis close?" Singh muttered.

"She's summoning up all her resources. Trying to distract him with sexual images while she fixes the knife—Oh, *God!*"

Everyone present, and Howson in his room high overhead, started at the moaning cry. Eyes rolling with terror, not seeing his surroundings but the fearful mental drama between Ilse and Phranakis, the watchdog gasped out the truth.

"She's weakening! She's losing control and he's creating guards for himself—schizoids, an army of them! He's made himself Cadmus and thrown down dragon's teeth and soldiers are springing from the floor!"

"Bring her back!" Singh cried, and knew even as he spoke that it was ridiculous. Someone—he didn't bother to notice who—put the fact into words.

"If you try and wake her now she'll leave half of herself behind, Pan. And she'd rather be dead than crippled."

So this was how it felt to lose. . .

She was very tired. It was almost a relief to feel her imaginary self pinioned by the arms, unable to struggle any longer. There were soldiers all around her, huge men with swarthy faces and coarse beards, armored with bronze and leather. Like a forest they stretched away under the dim roof of the marble hall. There had been a banquet, and a thousand revelers—puppets, a human setting for the glory of the master she had attempted to overthrow.

Had there been a banquet? Already she was uncertain where illusion ended; there was actual pain from the brutal grasp on her arms, and that made it difficult to concentrate. The world wavered. She was—she was—a captive. Yes; a condemned enemy, spared by clemency, caught in treachery. And her sentence was fixed, without appeal, by her intended victim.

Death.

Justice! approved the roar of a thousand voices, making her skull ring like the echoing marble roof. *Justice!*

Well, then—defeat. But it was not so strange after all. Indeed, in a way she had been defeated in everything she had ever tried, for no single task—a flood of memory welled up—no single task had ever been completed.

xiii

In incredulous horror Howson followed the decline of that bright glow of power which was now hardly to be called Ilse Kronstadt any longer. It was like seeing the last sparks die in a rain-swamped fire, knowing that the wolves waited at the edge of camp for the moment when they would be able to close in.

He was shouting aloud, in his little ridiculous piping voice, saying *NO NO NO* over and over; there were tears streaming down his cheeks because the mind of Ilse Kronstadt had been so beautiful, so clear and luminous, like the childhood image of an angel. Vandals were smashing the panels of stained glass, throwing dirt at the master painting, treading the tapestry into the mud. A madman was biting off the head of a baby, Time eating his children, blood dribbling down his chin, hoarse bubbling laughter making mock of human hopes.

And suddenly, without warning, like a last dry stick crackling into flame, the light returned. It showed a whole life, like a pathway seen from its end, with every step and stage of the journey clearly visible. Bewildered, awed, Howson gazed at it.

The flame began to die. There was a sense of illimitable regret—not bitter, because it was impossible for events to have gone otherwise. Gently resigned. Mists closed over the path, leaving only the failures as gray shadows in the gloom. So many of them; so many, many, many failures. And that one out of all: the symbol-child of fate, cursed lifelong by the heedlessness of a would-be tyrant, the selfishness of an ought-not-to-be mother, and the caprice of a cruel heredity.

The twisted baby whom I could not help . . .

He was blind, and yet he moved. Walked. Ran, his short leg dragging, finding somehow from somewhere the strength to open doors and go down winding stairs and traverse endless corridors he could not see for the tears that poured from his eyes, over his hollow cheeks. It was only his body that made the journey. He had gone elsewhere.

"Oh, my *God!*" said the watchdog, and came to his feet as though a vast hand had snatched him out of the chair. Singh shot out an arm to steady him, despair blackening his mind.

"Has she gone?" he whispered.

"Where's it coming from?" the watchdog cried. "My God, where's it coming from?" Like a cornered animal, he spun around, his eyes briefly mad with fear.

"What?" Singh shouted. "*What?*"

The technician watching the trace on the encephalograph gave a stifled exclamation. "Dr. Singh!" he snapped. "I'm getting an overlay rhythm! It's beating out of phase—and look at the *amplitude!*"

"Her heart's picking up!" reported another technician in an incredulous tone.

Singh felt his own heart give an answering lurch. There was no sense to be got out of the watchdog in his present state of shock, whatever had caused it; he hurried to stare at the encephalograph instead.

"See here!" The technician stabbed his finger at the weaving traces. "It's smoothing now, going into normal phase, but when it first came on it was heterodyning so much I thought she was done for."

"Is it Phranakis taking control of her entire mind?"

"It can't be!" the technician said with savagery. "I know his trace like—like his handwriting. And that's not his."

The air seemed to go stiff, as swiftly as supercooled water freezing. Totally lost, they looked at one another for an explanation.

"There's nothing we can do," Singh said at last. "We can only wait."

Slow nods answered him. And while they were still preparing themselves to endure the last crucial minutes, there came the noise from the passageway outside.

There were angry voices, raised to try and stop somebody. There were running feet, light and muffled on the sound-absorbent floor. There was a hammering on the outermost of the soundproof doors, and a thin, barely heard scream.

The watchdog, still in shock, made two steps toward the door, jerking like a badly manipulated puppet. Singh turned slowly, preconceived words about silence and danger dying as he sensed the truth and tried to remember what hope was like.

Then the doors slammed back and the giant came in, weeping, limping, and barely five feet tall.

There was the child, and I so wanted to help him, and I had to say those cheap rationalizing words about big problems and little problems. . . . The doctor said: one shoulder higher than the other, one leg shorter than the other—pretty much of a mess. And later I found out about his grandfather, and found it out from the woman's mind: she knew, and had the kid in spite of it, to use for blackmail. . . . Big problems! What bigger problem could there possibly be? And I so wanted to help, and my whole life has been like that because there are so many people sick and sad and I can help . . . could help . . . DAMN THIS LUMP IN MY BRAIN! No bigger than a bullet, and like a bullet it's killing me before I'm ready to die.

That was when Howson forgot himself.

At first she didn't understand the power that had suddenly come to her. It was like becoming a torrential river, vast and deep and terrible. It was raw because it was as new as a baby, but it *blazed*.

Life force. ??? No such—but: life force!

Defeat? DEFEAT?

There was no room left for ideas of death and defeat!

Slowly, calmly as she had considered the prospect of dying, she began to take charge of what she had been given. There was no resistance, and she never questioned the source of the power: she was too accustomed to meeting strangers in her own mind to waste effort in finding out. The fatal images forced on her by Phranakis receded, becoming ghostly-faint; she sensed his terror and immediately postponed consideration of it. She was a little frightened herself, but calm yet.

Seeking levers with which to direct the force, she found almost at once a familiar concept, and it related so strongly to her recent conscious preoccupations that she was shaken.

Mother-child: images of parturition, nourishment, support, warmth, love. Child-mother: images of reflected pride, hope, gratitude, love. The forms were ill-defined, as though from a source which knew little about such matters in real life. A faint puzzlement crossed her mind, and she dismissed it. With her detached consciousness she knew she had to make use of the power before she exhausted herself and lost her grip on it, and the first—the only—necessity was to struggle free of the hate Phranakis felt for her.

"She's breaking loose!" someone exclaimed.

"I saw her eyelids flutter," Singh whispered. There was a tightness in his chest he could not account for. His eyes were aching with the intentness of his staring; all his will was summed into the hope that his old, dear, marvelous friend should live. By what means she was rescued, he didn't care. Later—later!

"But she's *only* breaking loose!" muttered the technician by the encephalograph. "She isn't bringing Phranakis with her—No, wait a second!" He bent close to the Phranakis tape, as if he could see through the present and read what had not yet been recorded. "Something's happening, but heaven knows what!"

Cowed, bewildered, at a loss, the hero felt his satisfaction turn to ashes. A moment ago he was secure and confident; he had thwarted an attack on—well, his *life*, which sounded better than the truth, which was fearful to him. The last treacherous attempt of the barbarians to square accounts with him had been beaten off. The greatest city of all time, Athens the flower of civilization, was his, and its citizens were at his beck and call Through the centuries they would remember him, Pericles the Great!

Yet now he felt unreasoned terror. It seemed to him that he was darting about like a frightened rabbit, with a sword in his hand, looking for his enemies, hysterically defying them to come into the open. Out from the marble hall, out under the blue arch of the sky where he would roar defiance to the gods themselves if need be!

He threw back his head, filled his lungs, and could not speak. To his terror-stricken gaze it appeared that the sky rolled back, like a slashed tent, and the gods were manifest.

He wanted to fall on his face, bury his head in dirt, deny this as he had denied—what? Something terrible, but not as fearful as this! He was paralyzed. Whimpering, he had to look, and what he saw seemed to him to be the majesty of Zeus the Thunderer, who raised his bolt of lightning and cast it down on the mortal who had presumed to usurp the divine right.

Pericles the Great became Pericles Phranakis. Pericles Phranakis woke like a child screaming from nightmares, and those who watched over his body pounced to stop him from going back.

And Zeus the Thunderer, drained of all energy in a single terrific blast of mental mastery, fell headlong fainting to the floor.

"'Do we know how he did it?" muttered Danny Waldemar, looking down with incredulous awe at the limp little body in the hospital bed.

"The watchdog was too overcome to follow it exactly," Singh answered. He ached for Howson to recover consciousness; he knew he could never express his gratitude for sparing Ilse the humiliation of death in defeat, but he wanted the cripple to see it in his mind, at least. "We got a little of it. It was the sheer power that worked in the end, naturally; he was able to take anything Phranakis offered and turn it into some hostile, hateful image. I think he was babbling about the Greek gods when he woke up—perhaps he saw them when Howson broke into his fantasy. . . . Never mind; we'll know soon."

"What I don't understand is what persuaded him to help," Waldemar said. "I haven't contacted Ilse, of course; she's still so weak. . . . Do you know?"

"Yes, she was awake long enough to tell me while they were detaching the prosthetics." Singh paused and wiped his face. "It seems that Howson's father was Gerald Pond. Mean anything to you?"

"The—the terrorist? *That* one? Why, Ilse had to go and clear up after him when she was working for UN Pacification!"

"Exactly. And while she was probing wounded survivors for aggression data in a hospital there, she met Howson's mother. He'd just been born a few hours earlier.

"He's never been loved—do you know that? His mother had him to try and blackmail Pond into marrying her, and never cared much about him otherwise. And people have always seen his face first, and been—disturbed. So he's never been loved except once."

"Ilse?"

"Yes. She never saw him with her own eyes, which is why she didn't place him when he turned up here twenty-odd years later. But she saw him through his mother's mind a short time after his birth, and ever since then he's been a kind of symbol to her, summing up all the frustration she feels because she can't help all the people she loves. And she thought of him at what she expected to be the last moment."

"He was watching," Waldemar said. "We all were. When a telepathic force like Ilse's is fully extended, you can't avoid it. But I couldn't follow her down toward the dark. So I missed that. I was so . . . miserable I had to take my mind away, in case I weakened her."

"He not only stayed. He saved her."

"Will she be able to work again?"

"No. But she's going to live for a while. I'm sure of that. She's going to live long enough to teach Howson everything she knows."

"It's better than children," Waldemar said. "For us, I mean." He glanced at Singh. "Do you know that we envy you?"

"Yes," Singh murmured. "And we you."

"Including Howson?"

"No," Singh said. "He's never going to have it easy. He may find compensation in developing his talent, now he's exploiting it in a way that'll satisfy him. But he'll always have to fight his resentment of people who can walk down the street without limping and look others straight in the face."

Waldemar stared. Then he gave a chuckle. "I was going to tell you that," he said. "But if you've worked it out already . . . well, with you and Ilse to guide him, he'll survive."

"He'll do much more than just survive," answered Singh.

Book Three *Mens*

*B*ecause he was who he was, he had once asked for—and they had given him—a private aircraft to travel anywhere in the world, thinking to escape the dismayed stares and the whispering of ordinary people. But because he was what he was, even the faint shock which the pilot betrayed on meeting him hurt, and hurt badly. He bore with it for a little; then he cut short the trip and never asked for the plane again.

Because he was as he was, he could scarcely be alone. The next best thing was to be here at the therapy center in Ulan Bator, where those who knew him had outgrown their first instinctive reactions, and those who did not know him could assume he was a patient like themselves.

There had been certain changes in eleven years, but he was the same, even though he wore a different label now. He was Gerald Howson, Psi.D., curative telepathist first class, World Health Organization. He was one of the hundred least replaceable persons on Earth. It was good. It helped—a little. But he was still a runt, and his short leg still dragged as he limped through the corridors, and the same ugly face greeted him each morning in the mirror.

He had clung long to hope. He had remembered the deaf-and-dumb girl, given speech and hearing, and the way she came to thank him—him, Gerald Howson—with tears in her eyes. But that hadn't lasted. The visits grew fewer; finally they stopped, and he heard she had married a man from the city where he and she both had been born, and had children.

Whereas he was a hideous cripple.

There had been half promises—new techniques, new surgical processes. Once they had got as far as attempting a skin graft on him. But long before the slow-growing tissues had knit, before blood vessels could twine into the graft, it had gangrened and sloughed off. He was dully resigned by then. No matter how much thought he took, he could not add the wanted cubit to his stature; he was better employed any other way than pitying himself.

When the guards of consciousness were lowered by sleep, though, there was no escape if the lurking sorrows of the past chose to return.

Out of a dismal dream he snapped awake. *That* wasn't the usual imagery of his nightmares! He had them frequently enough to recognize their roots in real life, and nothing in what had startled him corresponded to direct experience.

He did not open his eyes. There was no point: the room was in darkness, and anyway the source of the signal which had stabbed into his brain was some distance away, partly masked by the "noise" of people dreaming. The message had loomed up suddenly like a shout from a quiet conversation. And it was a shout of terror.

Breathing evenly, forcing himself to remain relaxed, he sought identifying images in the mental flow. High mountains capped with snow, caravans winding through valleys, and the cadences of a language he did not understand. . . .

Got it—I think.

There was that Nepalese girl in Ward Four, the novice telepathist they had found too late, after her ignorant and terrified kinfolk had stoned her for a vessel of evil. She must be having a bad dream of her own.

Well, if that was the case, he could right matters without even leaving his bed. He made as though to contact her openly and soothe away her shapeless fear. One instant before revealing himself, he checked himself, and felt a frown draw down his eyebrows.

That wasn't Nepal, present time. Not even a country as isolated and mountainous as hers could be so primitive. Feudal customs? Magic? *Magic?*

He had sat up and thumbed the switch of the bedside intercom before he realized it. Waiting for an answer, he probed deeper into the extraordinary images echoing up to him. A sense of dependence and absolute mastery; a mood of defiant arrogance. *Those* weren't from the girl. And least characteristic of all was the feeling of masculinity coloring the thoughts. Like most people from a peasant background, she had rigid preconceptions of masculinity and femininity; she had conformed religiously to the social pattern at home in order to evade the worst consequences of her budding talent.

A tired voice spoke from the intercom. "Schacht here— duty doctor. What is it?"

"It's Gerry, Ludwig. Something's wrong with the Nepalese girl in Ward Four—something bad enough to waken me."

"Hmmm?" A wordless question as Schacht scanned the Ward Four tell-tale board. "I have nothing here from her. According to the tell-tales she's asleep."

"It's not original with her," Howson said. He was sweating; there was tremendous depth and complexity in the mental background of what he was picking up, and the more he groped into it the less sure he became of his ready-made explanations. Still, he had no better suggestion.

"Have we any male Chinese paranoids under therapy?"

"Yes; there's one undergoing coma and regression in the same wing as the girl." Schacht hesitated. "Not original with her, you said. Do you mean she's picking up the thoughts of an insane mind?"

"She's picking up somebody, and it's scaring hell out of her. Check the paranoid you mentioned. It might be him." He heard the doubt in his high-pitched voice.

"The chemotherapy tell-tales are blank, too. I thought the ego was completely masked in coma—out of reach."

"Maybe the depressant supply broke down. Check him anyway."

A pause. The impression of a shrug. "Very well. But if it isn't the Chinese paranoid, are you sure it can't be the girl herself?"

"Certain," Howson declared. "Hurry, Ludwig—please!"

"Gerry? He's totally unconscious. Are you *sure* it's not the girl herself—a schizoid secondary, maybe?"

Howson repressed an impulse to snap at him. He was sure, but he couldn't demonstrate why, using words. "Hang on," he said resignedly. So much for his chance of a night's unbroken rest!

He touched the control that moved the headboard of the bed into position as a contoured support for his deformed spine, and leaned back against its padding, staring into darkness.

First he would have to sort out from the inchoate succession of telepathic concepts some more clues than he had. Masculinity, Asian nationality, and enjoyment of power were hardly unique characteristics on this densely populated side of the planet. He surveyed the deeper levels cautiously. At least, he told himself, this didn't feel like the emanation of a sick mind. It wasn't even as irrational as most otherwise sane people became when they slept.

No; wait a moment. That must be wrong. He caught himself with a start. Hadn't there been referents in the very first contact which he'd defined reflexively as magic?

Growing more puzzled every second, he examined it closer. No good. It was blurred by the girl's incomprehension, and probably made unrecognizable. He'd have to look for the original source. In one way it shouldn't be too difficult: to reach into the awareness of a sleeping novice, the signal must be both close and powerful. But in another way the task was immense. "Close" could mean anywhere in the city, and there were a million-odd inhabitants.

"Gerry? You there?" Schacht demanded over the intercom.

"Shut up," Howson told him. "This feels big, Ludwig. Big—and bad."

He sensed Schacht's unspoken disbelief, and ignored it. Schacht at least made an attempt to master his instinctual revulsion against telepathists, and that was more than some people bothered to do.

He let his mind rove out over the night city, where a million brains made dreams sigh like the wind between tall white towers, down wide straight streets. That was a cosmopolitan consciousness, stranded together from all over the world and sometimes from farther away still—from the Moon, or Mars. . . .

He had rationalized his unwillingness to travel. Why go, when it all came to him? In this man's mind, a desert remembered; in that man's, a jungle; in another's, naked space, hurtful with stars sharp as knives.

But it wasn't a good rationalization. To live vicariously was to be a parasite, and even a symbiote could have little self-respect.

He jerked his train of thought back under control. He had had barely an hour's sleep before he was wakened, and he felt extremely tired. Nonetheless, he'd have to finish what he'd started before he could sleep again.

And all at once he had it.

"Got anything yet?" Schacht said with growing impatience. Howson barely heard the words; he was too depressed at the realization of what was happening.

"Gerry!"

"I'm—I'm listening, Ludwig," Howson forced out. "You'd better call Pan and get him to come up here, and Deirdre, too. And call an ambulance, and a car."

"What on earth have you found, then?"

"There's another catapathic grouping been set up. It's out in the city somewhere; I guess I can track it down." Images of absolute power, over natural law as well as men's minds, thrust the words down to second place in Howson's attention.

"Oh, marvelous!" Schacht said bitterly. "This is really my night! I've had two knife wounds, three burns, a car accident and two premature labors since I came on duty!"

Howson paid no attention. He was reeling under the violence of the events that were storming into his mind. Lacking any connection with external reality, yet charged with the full force of consciousness—as dreams, though equally illogical, never were—they gave him no fulcrum and no purchase. When he had viewed them through the intermediary mind of the Nepalese girl (who must have a sleeping pill to save her from this bombardment, he remembered dazedly), he hadn't realized the power driving them. And worse, there was this aura of perfect calm tinged with—with amusement. . . .

He exerted every ounce of will power and withdrew

from contact, trembling. He had driven his nails deeply
into his palms. Why should that surprise him? This was
what he feared most in all the world.

He spoke, both aloud and mentally, to the unknown
telepathist, putting all his hate and anger into a single
concept: *Damn you, whoever you are!*

Secure in fugue, pursuing a gaudy fantasy for his own
private reasons, the unknown might have sensed the signal and chuckled, inviting Howson to lay seige if he
wished to the fortress of his brain—or the idea might have
been Howson's own. He was too upset to tell which.

Agonized, he faced the inevitable future. No projective telepathist was worthless, and going by his current signals this man was exceptional among exceptions.
What intolerable strain had forced him to abandon reality
didn't matter; they would want him dragged back. They
would call on Howson, and because this was what he did
best in the world he would attempt it, and be sublimely
terrified, and maybe, this time, find that—

NO.

The order was to himself, but it was given as a deafening telepathic scream, and elsewhere in the hospital other
telepathists, including the Nepalese girl, reacted with
sleepy surprise. Blindly he reached to the shelf beside
the bed where he kept his stock of medicaments—he
was prey to as many emergencies as any patient in the
place—and found the tranquilizer bottle. He gulped two
of the pills down, and sat rock-still while they strait-
jacketed his writhing mind.

His breathing grew easier. The temptation to turn his
attention back to the glowing fantasies projected by the
unknown, receded, as though he had mastered the urge
to probe a rotten tooth and make it ache. When he judged
he was capable of movement, he got awkwardly off the
bed and reached for his clothes, preparing to go in search
of his anonymous enemy.

From the elevator he limped slowly down the main lobby of the hospital, passing the waiting emergency apparatus: oxygen cylinders on angular trolleys, like praying mantises, their shadows gawky on the cream-painted wall; wheeled stretchers with blankets neatly folded at the end; a machine called a heart, a machine called a lung, a machine called a kidney, as though one could take them, patch them together, and make a man.

With whose brain? Mine? I'd almost rather—

But the door had swung back, whispering with the rubber lip that kissed the rubber floor, and Pandit Singh was there in black sweater and gray pants, the light resting on his shock of hair like an aura.

"Gerry! What's this about a catapathic grouping? Brought in without notice? Where from? And what are you doing here, anyway? Isn't Ludwig Schacht on duty?"

The frost of fierceness in the words no more bespoke anger than the frost of gray on his bushy eyebrows bespoke age. He seemed changelessly young—on the inside, where it mattered. Promotion from his old post as head of therapy A to director in chief of the hospital hadn't altered him a jot. Howson had liked him on first meeting; now, after their long years together, he loved him as he would have wanted to love his father.

Once he had wished that his gift could be taken from him, to be abolished. The wish recurred occasionally, but now he would not have wanted to see it go from the world completely. Rather, he would have given it to Pandit Singh, as a man fit to wield such power.

Why me? Why me, the weakling?

He was dreadfully tired. But his thin voice was steady enough as he corrected Singh's mistaken assumptions.

"You must have come straight out without stopping to ask Ludwig for details, Pan. It's not that a grouping has been brought in. There's one out in the city. The Nepalese girl picked up some stray images in her sleep—it just happens that the setting of the fantasy corresponds to her own background—and I was wakened by her instinctive fear."

"I see!" Singh stroked his beard. "Can you locate them for us, or do we have to search?"

"Oh, I can track them down," Howson confirmed sourly. "That's why I got dressed."

Singh studied him for long seconds. Then, with one of his blinding bursts of insight, he said, "Gerry, it's not just that you haven't had your sleep. Is this an especially bad one?"

Miserably, Howson nodded. "It feels wrong, Pan. It hasn't got the right overtones of . . . weakness, or escape. I get an impression. . . . What the hell would you call it? Sardonic! Tough! Premeditated!"

Singh's mental reaction was grave. Yet it was somehow comforting, too; put into words, it might have gone: *If he's worried, he has good reason, so I can't contradict him. But he's the greatest; I know what he can do.*

Howson essayed a wry smile. The door of the lobby opened again, and Deirdre van Osterbeck came striding in, Singh's successor as head of therapy A—voluminous as a thundercloud in a great blue-black cloak, her face above it round and pale as the full moon. Ludwig Schacht emerged from the night office looking irritable, to announce that the car and the ambulance were on their way.

"Will one be enough, do you think?" he added, with a glance at Singh.

The automatic answer rose to Singh's lips: that there had never been a catapathic grouping consisting of more than eight persons, so one large ambulance and the estate car would suffice. Howson checked him, with a silent mental gesture.

"Make it two, Ludwig," he said. "I'm afraid that this man is breaking all the rules."

And to himself only, he repeated: *I'm afraid. . . .*

Fragmentary images tormented Howson as the car sped down the broad highway toward the heart of the city. They showed him bright impossible events which—if he let them—could displace reality forever. The hushing of their vehicle, the dark fronts of the buildings, the street lights, even the presence of other people near him would be blotted out, having no violence. Who could the unknown be? The submergence of real memory was so nearly total that Howson feared he might have to plunge deep, deep into the mental whirlpool before he found a clue. . . .

"Gerry!" Singh exclaimed. Howson caught himself. Without realizing, he had let himself drift.

"I'm sorry," he said thickly. "It's so strong. . . . I have to keep turning my attention on the source because I'm trying to locate it, and whenever I think in that direction I . . . I . . . Tell the driver to turn right, anyway. It's quite close now."

The car swung into a broad boulevard flanked by multistory buildings. Signs on their façades—red, green, blue—identified most of them as hotels.

"In one of these hotels, you think?" Singh suggested.

"Very likely," Howson murmured, the words drab with weariness.

"Then take your mind off the subject!" Singh snapped. "We can go from one to the next checking recent registrations. A few minutes' delay won't make any difference now."

"I can find them!" Howson protested. "Just a little—"

"I said take your mind off the subject! You're considerably too valuable to use as a bloodhound, hear?" Deliberately, Singh visualized a large, slobber-chopped, snuffling dog with its ears trailing so far along the ground that its frontpaws kept treading on them. Howson caught the image and had to smile.

You win.

The car pulled up at the curb. Singh opened the door, and Howson made to follow him out.

"No need for you to come, Gerry!" Singh objected.

"If I don't have something to distract me, I'm apt to . . . uh . . . revert to the subject," Howson countered. "I'm coming with you."

There followed half an hour of tramping along the sidewalk from hotel lobby to hotel lobby. Marble walls and plaques of artificial gems, mock animal skins rigged like a vast yurt, and illuminated tanks of green-dyed water witnessed a succession of sleepy night clerks raising their heads to stare in surprise at the intrusion of Howson and Singh, hesitating over displaying their registration lists, examining Singh's catch-all WHO authorization card, and yielding reluctantly.

Six hotels, and nothing to guide them. As they emerged from the latest of them and signified no progress to the anxious watchers in the car and ambulance at the roadside, Singh gave Howson a keen glance.

"Still keeping off the subject, Gerry?"

Howson gave an almost guilty grin. "How well you know me, Pan!" he replied with forced lightness.

"Well, stop it!" Singh said roughly. "If our man wasn't damned close you'd never have let me stop the car, and I can't think of a likelier place than a top hotel for an out-of-town telepathist to be found in. We'll probably get him at the next one we try."

The next one was decorated in a flamboyant Chinese rococo, with huge twisted brass pillars and red and black dragons lacquered on the walls. The night clerk was a stout middle-aged woman who kept one hand on an alarm button all the time she was talking to them; she was terrified of rape, and the concept flamed beacon-bright in her mind. Howson had to stifle a pang of disgust at the masochism which underlay her conscious terror.

Singh persuaded her to produce the file of registration cards, and riffled through a dozen or so before stopping, an exclamation rising to his lips. He snapped the important card from its holder and mutely showed it to Howson. In bold letters the name was inscribed: Hugh Choong.

"But he's—!" Howson began, and checked himself at Singh's frown. Wordlessly, he continued: *But he's a top, top man!*

Correct. Eleven years of close association with Howson had enabled Singh to verbalize an unspoken communication almost as clearly as a telepathist. *An arbitrator based on Hong Kong. Maintains the Pacific Seaboard beat virtually single-handed. Also a therapist retained occasionally by top UN staff. Not met him?*

No.

Nor have I. But we're about to, aren't we?

For the life of him, Howson could not have matched that mock-cynical comment. He felt only dismay. What was an arbitrator doing setting up a catapathic grouping? They were all chosen from the most stable, capable, highly trained telepathists; they had to be like Caesar's wife, beyond any breath of suspicion, for on the knife-edge of their self-control rested the uneasy peace of the planet.

If even such a man as that could choose fugue rather than reality, how secure was he, the cripple who could not even face strangers without being hurt?

Singh was speaking briskly to the night clerk. "Which is Mr. Choong's room, please? I shall have to disturb him."

"Mr. Choong's suite," the woman corrected morosely. "His party booked into our penthouse early this evening. But I don't think I can let you—"

"His party! How many?" Singh interrupted.

"Ten altogether." And unwillingly: "Sir."

"You were right about the need for another ambulance, Gerry," Singh grunted. "All right," he added to the night clerk. "Get a porter or someone to take us up—and hurry! It's a medical emergency, hear?"

Howson was content to comply with the course of events. He said nothing as he hobbled toward the elevator, in the wake of a porter wearing a sleepsuit and a startled expression. The ambulance attendants had gone around with their stretchers to the freight elevators. Howson left all that to Singh; he was busy trying to ride the bucking bronco of his thoughts, which threatened to run out of control whenever he let his attention wander toward the telepathic fantasies Choong was elaborating.

Try not to think of a white horse. . . .

The car stopped at penthouse level. Singh automatically made to use the passkey he had obtained from the night clerk, but the door opened before he applied it. And beyond . . .

"It reminds me," Singh said with ghastly calmness, "of the stage at the end of a performance of *Hamlet*."

Bodies everywhere! Only . . . not bodies, yet. Wax-pale, they sat or lay immobile, on chairs, couches, stacked cushions, nine of them in a circle around the tenth—a plump man with a Eurasian cast of features, relaxed in a padded armchair and wearing a splendid silk robe. At his side, as though this moment removed and set down, lay a pair of old-fashioned horn-rim spectacles. And that was, therefore, Hugh Choong.

Howson's fists clenched ridiculously. Like a badly jointed puppet he limped toward the trance-lost telep-athist, the violence of his anger fouling the air.

Damn you damn you damn you—

"Gerry!" Singh's words lanced into his brain. "You can't reach him, so don't waste the effort!"

Howson's rage, punctured, faded to nothing, leaving only a sick apathy. He made an empty gesture and turned his back.

"Where he's gone, he doesn't want anyone to reach him."

"I'm not so sure," Singh countered. "Look!" He strode over the soft carpet toward the wall-mounted phone and pointed to something on a low table close by. Howson's lackluster gaze followed him.

"There's a time switch on the phone, and it's set for eight tomorrow morning. And this is a recorder. Let's see what it says." He lifted up the small device, cased in a fine lacquered box, and discovered that it was connected to the phone by a gossamer-weight cord. A tug snapped the link; he depressed the replay switch.

At once a firm voice rang out.

"This is Hugh Choong in the penthouse. Good morning. Please do not be alarmed at this recorded message, which is set to repeat in case you don't take it all in at one go.

"Please contact the director in chief of the WHO therapy center, Dr. Pandit Singh. Inform him of my identity, and request him or one of his senior aides to come and see me. The elevator door is set to open automatically, so he will have no difficulty in entering. Thank you!"

"Shut it off!" said Howson savagely. "So he had it all worked out! The best of therapy, for no good reason!

And now, I presume—" He broke off, his mouth working.

"Yes, Gerry?" Singh prompted.

"You know exactly what I was going to say!" Howson flared. "Now somebody's got to go in after him, drag him out of fugue by force, waste time and effort that ought to go to somebody who needs it!"

"As far as I'm concerned, Gerry," said Singh in a tone he did not need to color with reproof, "the fact that Hugh Choong is here, in this state, makes him a person in need of therapy. Am I wrong?"

Howson flushed. He made as though to contradict, but before he had a chance to speak, the ambulance attendants came from the freight elevator, and Singh's entire attention went over to the supervision of their work.

Howson drew back into a corner out of the way, and gazed at the waxworn calm of Choong's face as they manhandled him on his stretcher.

No, damn you. That's why there's such a stench of smugness reeking around you! You can't have needed help, because you've taken so much care to make sure of getting it!

And you will, damn you again. They'll make me chase after you into that nowhere-land, destroy your dreams, pester and persecute you till you come back. And I'll take on the job, because this is all I have: my skill that nobody in the world can match.

So who will come after me, to help me, Choong? Who else is there? Damn you to hell.

xvi

His bitterness was still growing, accentuated by his lack of sleep, when the special conference convened the next afternoon. For any ordinary patient, a place on the regular daily agenda sufficed; for anyone else in UN employ, at most a multiline phone link

was used to discuss the case. But for Choong the high
executives came swarming in by Mach Five express.

In the chair reserved for him at Singh's right, he sat
trying to think of unimportant matters: the long low sea-
green ceiling, the exquisite crafting of the beechwood
furniture. He failed. He was much too aware of the guilt-
ily curious stares of the strangers, which asked as clearly
as a direct telepathic signal: *The world's greatest curative telepathist? Him?*

He could barely prevent himself from blasting at them
aloud: "What the hell did you expect, anyway? A superman? A pair of horns?"

Fortunately their attention had been distracted by the
arrival of copies of the physical-examination reports on
Choong and his companions. Now they were doggedly
plowing through a welter of detail, hoping to save themselves from asking ignorant questions later and looking
foolish.

Except one, he suddenly realized. Lockspeiser, the big
Canadian with the red face and the bald patch on his
crown, had shut his folder of papers and pushed it away.
That was an honest action, anyway. . . .

"Excuse me for being blunt, Dr. Singh," the Canadian
said. "But this stuff is for doctors, and I'm not one. I'm
an allegedly practical politician working with the Trade
Coordination Commission, and my interest in Dr. Choong
is confined to the fact that he was supposed to arbitrate in
the balance-of-credits crisis you may have heard about—
the Sino-Indonesian mess. It was hell's own job cooling
people's tempers to the point where they'd accept an outside referee, and they want Choong or nobody. That's
what counts with me. Can we skip the jargon and boil out
some hard facts now?"

So he *had* been running away from a job, had he? The
idea was oddly comforting to Howson. For seconds only,
though. Singh raised his head.

"Had he been notified that his services were required?"

"I don't know," Lockspeiser grunted. "I warned his
Hong Kong office, naturally. You're from there, aren't
you?" He glanced at the worried Chinese opposite him,
who had been presented to the meeting as Mr. Jeremy Ho.

"Yes. Ah . . ." He looked very unhappy. "The answer

to Dr. Singh's question is negative. We hadn't heard from Dr. Choong in over a week."

"And it didn't bother you?" Lockspeiser asked incredulously.

"Put it the other way around: we didn't—don't—bother Dr. Choong." Ho's tone was mildly reproachful. "We assumed he was making one of his regular study tours. He goes off to sound out public opinion, gathering background data which may prove useful in the future. Only he can say what's important to him."

Singh gave a polite cough. "I don't think we need pursue this any further. We've located Choong; our immediate difficulty is getting to him. We'd better concentrate on that."

"Agreed." That was the self-possessed woman with auburn hair, age—probably—thirty-five to forty, in black and green, who sat a little apart from her neighbor Lockspeiser. Her status was so far unknown to Howson, and he was curious about her. He was certain she was a telepathist, but when he had made the automatic polite approach to her, he had been met by a well-disciplined mental gesture equivalent to a cool shrug. It was effectively a snub, and it had upset him.

Singh blinked at the woman. "Thank you, Miss Moreno. Now, I understand from you that nothing of importance is known about Dr. Choong's companions. Correct?"

Miss Moreno gave an emphatic nod. "None of them has come to our attention previously," she confirmed.

"Our attention?" Howson said. All eyes switched to him, and instantly switched away again, except Miss Moreno's. Her answer was prompt and casual.

"World Intelligence, Dr. Howson."

Of course. When a man who holds the key to peace over a sixth of the globe defaults, you'd expect them to come running. Embarrassed at his own lack of perspicacity, and more troubled than ever at her refusal to acknowledge him on a telepathic level, Howson mumbled something indistinct.

Singh hurried on. "You've all been briefed on what's happened to Choong, naturally. What we can't figure out yet is why he's done it. We're analyzing the confidential psychomedical reports Mr. Ho brought from Hong Kong, but till we've done so we can only speculate. Before to-day I'd have said the reason for setting up a catapathic grouping was the same one for which any non-telepathist may go into fugue—to escape an unbearable crisis in real life. All our data, however, point to Choong being excellently adjusted, to his work, his private life, his talent. ... Yes, Miss Moreno?"

"Do we really have to prolong this conference?" the woman said brittlely. Howson tensed. For all her careful control, a leakage of indisputable alarm was reaching him. "There's only one course of action open and the sooner it's tackled, the better!"

Lockspeiser slapped the table with his palm. "Great! Will someone tell me *what* action? I'd never checked up on this—this catapathic thing before I heard about Choong. Seems to me he's blocked every way of reaching him . . . hasn't he?"

"What has to be done is this," Howson said in a voice as shrill and hard as a scream. "Somebody has to follow him into fantasy. Somebody has to risk his own sanity to work out the rules by which his universe operates—to sort out from ten real personalities and God knows how many schizoid secondaries the ego of the telepathist; to make the fantasy so uninhabitable that from sheer disgust he withdraws the links between himself and the others and reverts to normal perception."

He raised his eyes to meet Miss Moreno's directly. She gazed steadily back as he finished, "And it's not easy!"

"Did I say it was?" A hint of a flush deepened the olive tan of her cheeks.

"You said the sooner we tackled Choong the better." Howson parodied a bow of invitation. "You're welcome! For one thing, you have to learn your subject by heart first. If you don't, he can hide from you behind an infinite succession of masks, until you're too angry to outthink him, or too worn out to care, or—or too fascinated . . ." He swallowed and licked his lips, still looking toward Miss Moreno but no longer seeing her. "For another thing, while the body retains its energy reserves, an intruder has to slither in or not enter at all. If he's clumsy and obvious, he meets the combined resources of the participants head-on, and they deny his existence as they've denied their own bodies. This time there are ten in the grouping, and you may bet that Choong hasn't invited nincompoops and milksops to share his dreams! And lastly—" He stopped. They waited for him, the pause becoming like an interval between the lightning and the thunder.

"And lastly," Howson repeated very slowly, "Choong isn't an inadequate personality on the run."

Then why? Why? WHY?

He left them to get on with it after that. There were only the peripheral questions to settle, and it didn't matter who asked which; they were all predictable.

"Can't their resistance be lowered . . . by drugs, maybe?"

"Not by drugs. An electric shock to the organ of Funck is sometimes helpful. But any depressant we used would affect the motor functions—the heart, the breathing reflex—as well as the higher centers involved in imagination. We have nothing *that* selective on the nervous system."

"Well . . . prosthetic hearts, lungs?"

"No good until the telepathic linkage is already broken. Prior to that, they'd welcome it. It would mean that much less demand from their bodies, and the natural functions might cease for good."

"Does physical separation make any difference?"

"They use telepathists to communicate with Mars. I hope that answers your question!" Singh was getting edgy; his mind wasn't on the questioner, but on the absent Howson, wondering if he was eavesdropping from elsewhere in the building. He was, of course. He couldn't resist it.

Sensing the growing impatience of the director in chief, the others changed their minds about asking more questions, and Lockspeiser came straight to the point.

"All right, Dr. Singh! All that remains to be settled is this: will Dr. Howson tackle the job, and what are his chances of success in a reasonably short time?"

I wish I knew— But Singh masked that thought skilfully; maybe not even Miss Moreno detected it. He said aloud, "As to tackling the job: I'm sure he will. As to succeeding in a reasonably short time: he has an unbroken record of success in his previous cases, and few of his cures took more than forty-eight hours once they got started. Mark you, the ground has to be prepared, as he pointed out; he has to learn his patient from birth on, before he enters the fantasy."

"Fair enough," Lockspeiser grunted, and rose to his feet.

But Miss Moreno lingered, catching Singh's eye, and spoke when the door had closed behind Ho and Lockspeiser.

"I'm going to put that question again, Dr. Singh, if you don't mind. It's essential that we don't gamble in this matter. Are you *sure* Dr. Howson will get Choong back?"

Instantly, rage, as much as Pandit Singh ever allowed himself. And, spoken aloud: Don't let yourself say or even think that! Damnation, I've worked with Gerry for eleven years. I've seen him develop from a frightened, shy, retarded adolescent into a capable—hell, a brilliant! —therapist. His mind's as keen as a scalpel. I know that; how is it you don't? You're a telepathist yourself, aren't you?"

There was a moment of chill. Eyes closed, rocking a little on his special chair, Howson waited to feel Singh hear the answer. He had no wish to investigate Miss Moreno's mind if she had refused him contact previously.

Then: "How did you know? My office was under orders not to tell you, and I think I made it pretty clear to Howson that I—"

"I didn't have to be told!" Singh waved the words aside with an impatient gesture. "I've seen better than two hundred telepathists, sick and well, trained and novice. I still want an answer, though. How is it you don't know that Gerry is the one and only living man who can get Choong back?"

"Because . . ." There was a pause, colored by the gathering of will power toward a decision. "Because Choong scares me, if I've got to be frank! Ever since Vargas discovered the catapathic linkage, out of—I don't know— frustration, maladjustment. . . . Oh, skip that. Ever since, anyway, it's been a standing temptation to all of us. You're probably an exception if you've worked with so many telepathists, but most people imagine the talent is

absolutely rewarding and satisfying. For all the careful
propaganda to the contrary, they get jealous." The words
were bitter now. "Well, a telepathist can be frustrated,
or depressed, or lose heart. And any of us could say at
any time, 'Let the world go to blazes! I can make my own!'
But we're held back. We think, 'It's the weaklings who
give in!'

"But Choong has done it now. A weakling? *Him?* Never!
He apparently went into fugue by simple choice, in full
possession of his faculties. Is that where I'm going to end
up? Or Howson? Or all of us? I've been refusing rapport
with Gerry Howson, doctor. I know it's upsetting him.
But you see . . . I'm afraid that if I find he's as tempted
as I am, and if he finds I'm tempted, we'll have lost
not only Choong, but him, and me as well."

Singh had no answer. He merely bowed his head.

So there it was, in all its nakedness: the fear. Abruptly
Howson didn't dislike Miss Moreno any longer. She had
meant well. She had simply not realized that it was
more help to him to know that his terror was shared, rather
than a product of his individual plight.

How had Marlowe put it in the mouth of Mephistoph-
eles? Something about it being sweet to have companions
in adversity? He couldn't remember. It didn't matter. The
principle applied, and he felt comforted.

His hand went to the switch of the intercom. A pause,
and then Deirdre van Osterbeck spoke.

"Yes?"

"Gerry here, Deirdre. Send me the background on the
Choong case, please. I'm ready to start work on it now."

xvii

Usually he relied at least in part on inspiration to
achieve his ultimate success. Many times in the
past he had brought about a swift and drastic dis-

ruption of a catapathic grouping by exploiting a weakness revealed only in the fantasy itself, never previously admitted by the telepathist even to his analyst, even to his wife—if he had a wife; rather few telepathists bothered to marry, in view of the unlikelihood of their having children with the gift.

This time, however, nothing was left to last-moment improvisation. He employed every trick in the book.

First there were the long, long hours under the hood—the close-fitting device combining microfilm viewer, microphone and audible commentary outputs. He used a mild stimulant to help him fix the endless facts in his brain, and came out from each session limp and sweating.

Then there were the direct investigations. They brought him anyone and everyone they could find who had known Choong at all closely: former schoolfellows, elderly relatives, ex-girl friends, professional colleagues—in all more than two hundred minds for him to dip into, sift, pick clues and hints from.

Last, they brought Choong's wife.

He had not wanted to face her. He had tried to tell himself, her and Singh that it wasn't necessary, he had enough material to satisfy him. But in the end he had to accept the ordeal. She herself insisted. She wanted her husband back, and if her memory held anything of use to Howson, she wanted him to have it.

She was a small woman, pudgy, not very attractive, a receptive telepathist of fair accomplishment. Her ancestors were mostly Polynesian, but her present work was largely concerned with cultural adjustment in New Guinea, cushioning the impact of modern technology on people whose grandfathers had been born in the Stone Age. She had been away working for more than three months, and had not expected to see her husband again for another six weeks.

When Howson first probed her, he was already convinced of what he would find. Here if anywhere must be the intolerable situation Choong was running from, surely! He looked for the signs of marital, probably sexual, strain —and was bewildered.

They weren't there. He found only a hurt puzzlement, a mute question: *why did he go without me?*

And she didn't know the answer, even when he burrowed into the chaos of her subconscious. To all outward and *inward* appearance, Choong was the best-adjusted telepathist Howson had ever run across, and his adjustment to his wife was as good as any other part of his existence.

Shaken, he resisted the growing impulse to cut short his preparations. He knew Lockspeiser and Ho were getting anxious; he knew even Singh, whose confidence in him was tremendous, had started to wonder whether these elaborate precautions were necessary or just an attempt to postpone the eventual therapy. Not even if the Sino-Indonesian crisis flared into violence would he dare to face Choong without knowing his weak points.

And since Choong didn't have any, to speak of, that left his companions.

Here the task was infinitely easier. Although none of these nine people would have succumbed to escapist fantasy of their own accord, they had required little persuading to join with Choong. Consequently he found hopeful indications in their psychological records.

This man: repressed will-to-power, king-and-slave fantasies revealed in analysis a few years earlier.

And this man: a childhood history of lying, petty theft and furniture-breaking.

And this woman: attempted suicide after an unhappy love affair.

I'm a ghoul, Howson thought, not for the first time. *Here are people at the end of their tethers, and in despair they've tried to break loose. So what do I do? I play on their private misery, and make even escape unbearable.*

"Set them up, Deirdre. I'm on my way down now."

"Good! We'll be ready when you arrive; I've had staff standing by all day."

Howson turned off the intercom, got to his feet and stretched. He wished he could stretch completely, and tense the withered muscles of his back, which had never been drawn out. Still, wishing was futile. He ought to have learned that by now.

His mind buzzed with the information he had packed

into it over the past few days as he limped through the corridors toward the room where his patient waited. It was like being pursued by hornets.

Moreover, there was memory to dog his footsteps. Maybe it was a mistake that he had never moved from the room he was first assigned when he came here. Maybe he should have gone to an apartment out in the city. Then he wouldn't now be walking the same route he had followed, blind with tears, when Ilse Kronstadt came so near to death in her encounter with Pericles Phranakis.

Was this his own hour of crisis? Ilse, too, had had an unblemished record, until (what had she compared it to?) the bullet-sized tumor in her brain weakened her. His physical powers were no worse than they had ever been, but his control had nonetheless been subtly undermined, for just the reasons Miss Moreno had confided to Pandit Singh. He was embarking, scared, on an enterprise in which only the most sublime confidence in his own ability could uphold him. And there was no reluctant novice to come storming to his rescue at the eleventh hour.

It'll come to teamwork eventually: we'll have to take two or three low-grade projectives and maybe use hypnosis to subdue their individual egos, and put a curative telepathist in command, and— But that's a catapathic grouping, almost!

No, that wasn't the answer. Not yet. Not until the process of assimilating telepathists into a world run by ordinary people was complete. And by then, maybe, there wouldn't be the pressure on telepathists which drove them into fugue, anyway.

Maybe there would only be cases like Choong's. . . .

He came into the room where they awaited him, and looked around, nodding. He hadn't carried out a preliminary sweep of those present—he was preoccupied with his own worries—so it came as a surprise to see that Miss Moreno was here. He glanced at Singh, asking a wordless question.

She answered him directly, before Singh could speak.

I'd like to watch you, Dr. Howson. I'm so impressed by what I've learned from Dr. Singh.

"Well, well!" Howson spoke aloud by reflex. "What a change there was!" He looked steadily at her, and saw her wince, but she kept her mind open. It was a good, sinewy impression he received: stable, resilient, in some ways comparable to Choong's but with a strong feminine component.

"I see," he said finally. "It's to impress on me that not all telepathists have gone the way Choong chose to go. Rather elementary: I mean, here we are, after all. . . . But watch all you like. Just don't, whatever happens, try to take a hand."

He didn't wait for an answer, but moved to the bed. An attentive male nurse made as though to help him. It wasn't necessary; this was perhaps the thirtieth time he had taken his place for such a task. He looked around as the various machines were disposed on his body.

There had been very few changes since he first saw this room, he reflected. Experience had suggested improvements in the layout; there had been developments in medical technology, and superior recording devices and superior prosthetics had replaced the ones from Ilse Kronstadt's day. That apart, the scene was essentially identical to the setting for his introduction to his career.

He looked at Singh, who gave him a big smile half-swamped by beard and mustache. He looked at Deirdre van Osterbeck, who was too busy checking the encephalographs to notice. In both their minds he sensed a conflict between hope and anxiety.

The therapy watchdog—a tubby young man with slanted eyes and a fixed mechanical smile, named Pak Chang Mee—settled in his chair next to Howson. He had worked with Howson twice before, and a quick mental scan revealed that he was extremely confident of success.

And there was Choong.

"Ready," Deirdre said curtly. The technicians echoed her, nodding to Singh. At the back of the room near the door Howson sensed Miss Moreno composing herself in a soft chair; he did not see her move, for he had already closed his eyes.

"Record now," he said. Images welled up, the instant he began to relax toward contact. "I'm getting the main pattern—the city, the mountains. . . . I reported winter previously. That's fading. The scene is being set for some big event. I shall try and go in along fringe path K, the

trade and travel path. Caravans come to the city and I
have detected at least one schizoid secondary of very
high order using that as a background."

He had probed Choong cautiously a score of times
while he was building up his store of information. Now
the imaginary world seemed familiar, almost welcoming.
Knowledge of the hospital faded, and there was only . . .

xviii

. . . the rocking motion, like a small boat on a choppy
sea, and a smell like no other smell that ever was.

Camels. He opened his eyes. The illusion was absolute,
but he had not expected it otherwise. He was dealing, after
all, with a brilliant opponent.

By degree facts sorted themselves out. He was . . . he
was Hao Sen the mercenary, the caravan guard, and he
rode negligently on his magnificent she-camel, Starlight,
alongside the motley gang of traders and travelers
through the gates of Tiger City. The air was sharp and
stimulating; the winter was almost over, and this was the
first of the spring caravans to brave the bandits and cross
the mountains from the north.

Bandits . . . The concept brought a sense of weariness
and satisfaction, and he remembered. There had been
fighting; the bandits had laid an ambush. Signs were all
around him: that man was limping, and that one had a
bloody bandage on his head. He himself—he tensed his
square-set muscular body—had not a few bruises where
his armor of brass plates on leather had turned a sword
cut. But they had won through, and this summer, said
the common gossip, the Emperor would raise an army
and smoke the bandits out of the hills for good and all.

He yawned cavernously behind his spade-shaped black

beard. His hand fell to the familiar hilt of his short broad sword, and he urged his camel on toward the city gate.

The walls were huge and solid; the black puppet-forms of soldiers tramped back and forth along them. Above the gate itself was a balcony on which were ranged shields bearing the stylized black-and-yellow emblem of a tiger's head. This was magical protection, wisely chosen; the city was impressive, and deserved that the name of the second most powerful beast in the world be bestowed on it. (Where had he learned that? Who had told him that the ancient Chinese so regarded the tiger? He frowned for a moment, and then had to set the question aside for consideration.)

Now the populace were coming down to the street inside the gate, cheering and waving, and some tumblers near the head of the procession turned wild handsprings to return the greeting. Hao Sen gave a booming laugh at their antics, and eyed the moon-faced girls as he passed, like any soldier who had spent a long time without women.

There were city guards in squads to direct the caravan and clear its path; there were sharp-nosed merchants closing their houses to get down to the market and snap up bargains. There were touts for local taverns, there were —oh, a myriad different people assembling.

Into the great market place they poured to the accompaniment of shouts, firecrackers, brazen gongs. Hao Sen rode steadily at walking pace, absorbing all possible information about his environment.

He was shaken by its detail. This was—fantastic!

"You there!" A booming bass voice penetrated his reverie, and an officer of the city guard, splendid in magical black and yellow, came striding toward him. "Dismount at once! It's not permitted to ride any beast through the market."

Hao Sen grunted and complied. That was irritating, but he dared not object: it was far too early to start drawing attention to himself. Starlight showed her opinion with the derisory curl of the upper lip which passes for expression among camels, and he failed to repress a grin.

"What's to be done with my camel, then?" he demanded.

The officer pointed a short distance back down the way he had come.

"You'll find taverns there, with stables to your liking. I'd hurry if I were you, or all the places will be taken."

A short time later, on foot, his sword clinking at his side in its leather-and-brass scabbard, he returned to the marketplace. It was a scene of tremendous activity now; the loads from the pack animals of the caravan had been spread out around three sides of the square, for purchasers to inspect, and booths had sprung up everywhere in the center: barbers importuned passers-by to have their hair trimmed and their noses and ears cleaned out, conjurers, tumblers and jugglers were practicing their skills, musicians had taken station and launched into wailing song to the accompaniment of twanging moon-guitars. Among the crowd Hao Sen wandered at random, a frown etched deep into his forehead.

The fourth side of the square, the one from which the traders had been kept away, was nonetheless busy. On to it fronted a vast building with twenty pagoda-curved roofs and a flight of probably a hundred steps leading to its main doors. In red and gold ideograms on the façade there was spelled out its title: THE TEMPLE OF HEAVENLY FAVORS.

On the steps, a gang of workmen were busily completing a dais for a throne. Hao Sen contemplated them. From the gaudy silk hangings they were draping over their work, a visit from the Emperor was anticipated.

The assumption was confirmed when he noticed that there was a stout man making a circuit of the market, accompanied by armed guards, and pointing out items of specially choice nature for the merchants to hold back from their stock. Some of these items were being collected by grunting youths in grimy white clothing and toted across the square to the foot of the steps before the temple.

The Emperor. Hao Sen contemplated the chance that the obvious focus of his attention was the real ruler. He decided against the possibility; at least one of the reflective personalities involved in this superb imaginary city had had king-and-slave fantasies, and the Emperor was more likely to be a subsidiary than a main personality.

On the other hand, of course—

Hao Sen checked his train of thought with a start. He had just caught sight of a dragon-trainer between two colorful booths across the square.

He shouldered his way toward the spectacle, ignoring the objections of those he pushed aside, and halted at the front of the ring of watchers surrounding the trainer and his beast. They were keeping a respectful distance.

Not that this was much of a dragon. It looked half-starved, and was barely three-quarters grown; moreover, its scales were patched with a mildew-like fungus disease. Its vicious three-inch teeth, nonetheless, were white and sharp as it bared them in effectual snarls. The trainer—a thick-set, swarthy man, probably a gypsy from the south—was making it move its legs in a kind of clumsy dance, goading it with a pointed ankh which he heated at intervals in a brazier.

Hao Sen shivered as he watched, not at the baleful threat in the beast's eyes, which promised it would not stand for much more such treatment, but at the significance of the disease afflicting it.

While he was still reflecting on the implications, there was a blast of trumpets from behind him, and he turned. A procession of gorgeously uniformed soldiers was striding into the square, followed by men bearing a palanquin of rich silk and rare woods. Officers bawled for the proper respect to the Emperor, and like a forest felled at a single blow, everyone in the square dropped into the imperial kowtow.

When permission was given to rise, the Emperor was in place on his throne, surrounded by his train: mandarins of the peacock feather, personal servants with symbolic fans, and high officers of his army. Hao Sen scanned them with interest. His attention was drawn almost at once to a tall man in magnificent silken robes standing at the Emperor's right, a little apart from the rest and apparently having no personal attendants with him.

Somehow that . . . smelled right. Hao Sen ignored the business which followed, the presentation of the caravan master and the display of choice goods to the Emperor, and studied the tall man. There was no overt resemblance, but that was hardly evidence. Consider, after all, his own body now. . .

He broke off that thought with an almost physical jolt, and wondered whether it was still too soon to draw attention to himself. On the one hand, the completeness of the detail was a sign for caution; on the other, it implied that the secondaries were exceptionally well developed. He had arrived, in his own chosen disguise, and so far no hint had been given that his presence was suspect. . . .

He made up his mind, and worked forward through the crowd to the front row of those who had forgotten the attractions of the conjurers and mountebanks for the privilege of seeing the Celestial Emperor at close quarters. By now the Emperor had completed his inspection of the caravan master's wares, and was leaning back on his throne casually eying the scene. It was a matter of moments before he caught sight of Hao Sen and said something to the caravan master.

"Why, we owe him a great debt!" the caravan master exclaimed. "He it was who chiefly inspired our guard to repel the bandits."

"Let him come forward," the Emperor said negligently.

An officer signaled to Hao Sen, who obediently marched to the foot of the steps and dropped on his knees in the kowtow. Directly he had completed the obeisance, he rose and stood with his hand on his sword and his shoulders thrown back.

The emperor looked him over. "A good fighting man," he said with approval. "Ask him if he plans to join my army."

"Celestial Master, your humble servant hears that the army will go forth this summer against the bandits. If he is granted the privilege of joining the enterprise, he will serve with all his heart!"

"Good," said the Emperor briefly. His eyes lingered a moment on Hao Sen's brawny frame. "Take his name, one of you," he added. "And convey me back to the palace."

Mechanically Hao Sen complied with the request of the officer who came to take his name and details of his experience. This was a routine precaution; if he was reduced to stripping away the reflectives one by one, he now had the background for turning a king-and-slave fantasy into something altogether less palatable. But he was satisfied the Emperor himself was only a reflective.

Then was the real ruler that tall man, standing apart? Or someone else, not engaged in this subsidiary part of the drama?

Once more, he postponed a decision.

The imperial procession had left the square when the shout went up.

"The dragon! The dragon!"

He spun around, seeing a wave of catastrophic panic break across the market like a bore in a river mouth. Buyers, sellers and entertainers alike streamed outward from the square, overturning booths, scattering merchandise and trampling old people and children in the rush. Hao Sen stood his ground, waiting for a clear view.

When he got it, he was chilled. The dragon was no longer sullenly submissive. It was an incarnation of menace. On three of its sharp-taloned legs it stood over the corpse of its former master, slashing at his face and turning it to bloody ruin.

It tired of its play, and paused, its yellow eyes scanning the great square. Hao Sen had half expected it to feed, for it would certainly have been kept hungry to weaken it. Yet its head did not dip to gnaw the corpse, and his heart gave a lurch as he realized that the square, apart from himself, was now completely empty.

He might have run. He had delayed too long. The slightest move would attract its attention, and somehow he was sure it could catch him, no matter how fast he fled. The reason why he had been made to leave his camel out of the square struck him like a blow. He had used his favorite trick once too often, and here was an opponent who employed it himself.

The dragon began to move, sidling toward him, its eyes unblinking and burning bright as the coals of the brazier it had overturned. Hao Sen glanced frantically around for a weapon. He saw the broken shaft of a tent close by, and jumped for it. The instant he did so, the dragon charged.

He hurled the tent pole javelin-fashion and dropped on his face. More by luck than accuracy of aim, the sharp wood hit fair on one of the mildew-weakened patches of scales. It made a barely noticeable gash, but the dragon howled with pain. It spun around and returned to the attack.

The first time he threw himself aside, dragging out his sword. The second time, he failed to dodge completely; the beast cunningly curled its tail in midair so that it caught his shoulder and the blow sent him sprawling. That tail was like a club, and the dragon must weigh as much as a man.

It landed now among a tangle of cords on a rope seller's stall, and was hindered long enough for Hao Sen to devise a tactic to meet its next pounce. This time, instead of leaping sideways, he flung himself backward, in the same movement bringing up his sword point foremost so that it sank into the dragon's underbelly.

The hilt was wrenched away with such force that it nearly sprained his wrist, and the impact made his head ring as it hit the paving. Shrieking with agony, the dragon scrabbled with its clawed hind feet, and a triple line of pain told him where the slashes penetrated his leggings.

He brought up one booted foot with all his force and kicked at the base of the beast's tail. That hurt it sufficiently for it to forget him momentarily, while it doubled its neck back under its body and tried to pull the sword out with its teeth. Dark blood leaked down the hilt, but slowly.

Hao Sen rolled clear instantly. He considered attempting to gouge out the dragon's eyes, but they were shielded by bony orbital ridges; he was more likely to lose his fingers. Desperately he sought a weapon to replace the lost sword, and saw none. The dragon abandoned its futile tugging at the sword, snarled, leaped again.

It came at him crookedly because the blade in its belly weakened one of its hind legs; nonetheless, its heavy tail curved toward his head in what threatened to be a stunning blow as it passed him. Gasping, Hao Sen seized the tail in both hands—and began to spin on his heels.

For one fantastic second he thought it was trying to climb down its own tail to get at him. Then the weight on his arm gave place to an outward tug. Four times—five—the market whirled dizzily; the dragon's blood spattered an ever wider circle on the ground. He added one last ounce of violence to its course, swinging it upward, and let go.

Across the rope seller's stall it flew, over the spilled coins to the booth of a money changer, and fell, its head twisted at a strange angle against the lowermost of the temple steps.

Hao Sen dropped his aching arms to his sides, panting. He looked at the dragon's carcass, and beyond it, up the steps, until he met the gaze of the tall man who had stood there watching, leaning on a staff.

And then he knew.

xix

A good fight," the man with the staff said in a tone calculated to suggest he had seen a dozen such. Hao Sen made no reply; his heart was hammering too violently. All his plans had gone to nothing now. He was utterly vulnerable.

His only hope was to try and maintain the fiction that his guise was merely the effect of the creation of a schizoid secondary personality in the general run of the fantasy. He spat in the dust, rubbed his hands together, and went over to the dragon to draw his sword from its belly.

A glance showed him it was useless; the hilt was bent at right angles to the blade. Cursing, he made to toss it aside.

"Wait!" said the man on the temple steps in a commanding tone. "A sword that has taken the life of a dragon is not a weapon to discard so lightly. Give it here."

Reluctantly Hao Sen complied. The man took it and examined it carefully; then, muttering something Hao Sen could not catch—a charm, presumably—he made a ring of his thumb and first finger, which he ran the length of the staff he carried. He kept the ring closed while he put the staff in the crook of his elbow and grasped the sword hilt with his free hand. Then he passed the ring down the blade.

The blood curdled and fell away, leaving the metal bright. When he reached the point where it was bent, it first quivered and then sprang to straightness, singing.

"I am the wizard Chu Lao," said the tall man in an offhand voice. "Here, take your sword!"

And the second after, he was gone.

Bleakly Hao Sen considered the facts as they presented themselves. They made a depressing total.

It was clear that for all his careful preparations he had made one hidden and potentially fatal assumption: that he was dealing with an opponent like his other opponents. He was *not*. He was up against a man capable of taking just such thorough precautions in the elaboration of his fantasies as in any other department of his existence. The patch of mildew on the flank of the dragon should have been warning enough. Detail like that was almost inconceivable unless it was a product of Hao Sen's reaction with his environment, or the dragon was a schizoid secondary, not a construct.

He'd used that trick himself often enough; he had been planning to use it again when he conceived the camel Starlight. And whether by guesswork or foresight, he'd had that gun spiked at once.

So the dragon had been a schizoid secondary, with its own "real" personality. And the master of Tiger City was not the Emperor, luxuriating in pomp and adulation. He was Chu Lao, the wizard.

Wizard! He shivered. No wonder the very first breaths of this fantasy had borne to him suggestion of magic!

True, he remembered previous occasions on which there had been magic incorporated into a world-picture. But then he had found it to be mere childish grandiosity, hastily cobbled together and lacking coherence. The magic practiced by Chu Lao, on the other hand, would be consistent, rigorous, governed by carefully worked-out laws; it would be as rigid and inflexible as science. And Chu Lao knew those laws. Hao Sen didn't.

He abandoned his original plans completely. Not for him now the subtle undermining, the fencing for a chance to seize control, which had been his favorite technique in the past. To use the weapons forged by his enemy and fight on ground chosen by him—that was a certain path to exhaustion and defeat. He looked over the sword the magician had mended for him, his thoughts grim.

At all costs he must avoid defeat. To be beaten once would be an irrevocable sentence of doom.

Yet somehow he must still work within the pattern set by his opponent; to disturb the basic hypotheses too drastically would give a chance for the mental rapport to be broken, and he might find himself wandering in a fantasy world of his own création, in which he was deluded into believing he had actually succeeded, whereas all the opposition he had overcome consisted in straw men. . . .

He reached his decision. Brute force was the only chance he now had. Then let it be by force.

They came down from the hills, purposefully, in ordered ranks: no barbarian rabble, these bandits, but an army welded together by discipline into a single efficient machine. When they were still miles from Tiger City, the glint of morning sun on their shields and helmets caught the attention of the city guards, and at once there was a great running to and fro on the ramparts.

Riding easily on his camel at the head of his army, Hao Sen grinned into his beard. His long pike with its cruel head was couched in its rest, alongside Starlight's stately neck; his sword tapped lightly on his thigh.

Let them fuss and flurry! It would do them little good. What he had in store was enough to shake everyone in Tiger City up to and including the arrogant Chu Lao.

For more than an hour the bandits tramped down from the hills, silent except for the banging of gongs which marked the step. They made no attempt to come within bowshot of the city, but followed the circumference of a circle and surrounded it. Pack animals laden with brushwood, wagons with dismantled siege-engines, and great store of food added up to an obvious conclusion: they were determined to besiege the city before the Emperor could equip his army and provide adequate forage for his planned campaign against them.

Pleased, Hao Sen studied his work. He had chosen a comparatively minor post for himself, at the head of a detachment of camel cavalry, and the apparent chief of the bandits enjoyed all the luxuries a horde such as this could afford: a huge traveling yurt gorgeous with fine furs and pieces of stained Turkey carpet, on a four-wheeled wagon drawn by ten oxen. Around the wagon buzzed a continual swarm of officers, messengers and slaves.

The army halted. On the ramparts of the city were visible the leaders of the defending force. After a while, these collected on the balcony over the main gate, opposite which the chief's wagon had taken station.

A herald went down to begin the formal preliminaries by demanding the surrender of the city without resistance. The answer was dignified but negative. It was followed by a shower of arrows, and the herald rode hastily back to his lines.

Fair enough. Hao Sen watched the defenders duck as the fire was returned. Then there was an interval punctuated only by desultory shots while messengers brought in information about the defenses.

It seemed that the main gate was the only vulnerable spot. Accordingly, the bowmen kept the heads of the defenders down while loads of brushwood and pots of pitch were dragged toward the heavy wooden doors closing it. Several men fell, but the job was well under way when it was abruptly abandoned. The attackers drew back, and the surprised defenders took stock of the situation. Cautiously they peered out from behind the black-and-yellow tiger's-head shields to see what had changed the minds of the bandits.

The answer was soon apparent. The sky was clouding over rapidly, and a few drops of rain were spitting down already. No fire fierce enough to harm the gate could survive such a downpour as was threatening.

Hao Sen stared narrow-eyed toward the balcony over the gate. Surely that was—yes, indeed! There was the wizard Chu Lao, in a dark cloak that almost blended with the stone wall behind him, staring up toward the oncom-

ing clouds. His magic was being called on to defend
the city, and so far it looked as though he had the upper
hand.

Hao Sen gave another wolfish grin, and the attackers leaped into action.

The furs and gaudy hangings on the "chief's wagon"
were snatched aside, revealing that they covered only a
light bamboo frame with enough space for a man to enter,
wait as if talking to the chief, and turn around to leave
again. Apart from that, the whole wagon was an incendiary machine, full of tinder, pitch and jars of oil.

Now they whipped the only pair of oxen which had
not been unharnessed. The startled beasts bellowed and
leaned on the traces; the wagon rolled. After ten yards
men dashed in with swords and slashed the oxen free,
and the wagon continued by itself down the sloping road
to the gate, its wooden wheels rumbling.

Hao Sen waited tensely. The defenders had seen what
was happening, and were scrambling frantically to get off
the balcony over the gate.

Another ten yards . . .

The fire-arrows went whizzing after the wagon; the
second and third struck fair on oil-soaked rags at the back
of the inflammable pile, and flames soared twenty feet,
crowned with licking black thunderheads of smoke. The
wagon slammed into the gate with a crunch of collapsing
boards, and at once there was an inferno.

So far, so good. But had Chu Lao been taken unawares?

Apparently not, for the rain came streaming down after
only a few minutes' hesitation. As the smoke and flames
died, it could be seen that a wide gash had opened in the
gate. Another incendiary wagon was being readied at
the head of the slope to follow the first when the gate
was hurled open and the defenders charged out in force.

This was such an illogical act that Hao Sen was startled. Tiger City's best strategy would clearly be to wear
the attackers down—or so he had thought. For a moment
he questioned his own planning; then the city guards,
both mounted and on foot, were streaming forward with
yells and much brandishing of swords, and there was no
time to wonder about second-best courses of action.

The fighting spread by degrees all around the city. It was tough work. After a while Hao Sen spotted a large silken banner being borne forward from the gate, and he dismissed his own command into the charge of a junior officer whom he suspected of being one of his schizoid secondaries. That banner was embroidered with a tiger, and must belong to the Emperor.

No! Wait!

Sudden insight, as blinding as lightning, pierced the gray, sober mood of Hao Sen's mind. The tiger banner couldn't be the Emperor's; the imperial symbol was the dragon, the most powerful of all beasts. So the tiger would be reserved to Chu Lao, the wizard, because this was his city —Tiger City—and magic operated here according to strict rules, of which he had seen an example when Chu Lao repaired his sword and told him that a weapon that had killed a dragon was worth keeping. . . .

And the tiger was only the *second* most powerful beast!

Hao Sen urged Starlight forward, his mind racing, trying to beat his path to the spot where the tiger-gaudy banner was set up.

There was a violent melee all around it, so it was a while before he could reach a spot from where he could see if indeed Chu Lao had come out to supervise the battle. Three times he had to use his pike to spit a construct soldier, and the third time he lost his grasp on it; shocked, because that implied he was much more tired than he had believed, he took a firm grip on himself as well as his sword.

At the same moment he saw the wizard under his banner, and the wizard saw him. Instantly, guards formed to block his path. Hoping that Chu Lao's attention was distracted, he hurled himself sideways from his saddle, and Starlight rose on her hind legs, kicking furiously. The guards went flying.

The camel afforded only an instant's respite, though. She was slashed across the forelegs the moment she touched ground with them. Hao Sen ignored her dying wails and fought onward, his sword sweeping an arc of death. Twice glancing blows made his helmet ring; twice he felt his sword-point slow and then free itself in a manner that meant it had cut clean through flesh. A dismembered arm seemed for one wild moment to be trying to catch hold of him by the beard.

Then he was through, and into the circle of enchanted ground surrounding the wizard.

"Chu Lao!" he shouted. "Chu Lao!"

The wizard, astonished, gazed at him—and yet that wasn't only astonishment. There was . . . sardonic amusement. . . .

Hao Sen rushed on "Chu Lao, *I name your city!*"

All over the battlefield men seemed to lose heart for the fight. As though struck by a premonition, Chu Lao wavered.

"The city is Tiger City! That tiger *is* your city! And the tiger is less powerful than the dragon!"

How it happened could not be seen, but where the city had stood was a green-eyed striped cat, crouching and snarling, its claws unsheathed and huge beyond imagining.

"My tiger!" cried Chu Lao. "Yes, that is my tiger!"

"And this sword has drunk a dragon's blood!" Hao Sen shouted. *"This sword is my dragon!"*

He whirled the blade once around his head and flung it sparkling into the air; as it twisted, it changed, and as it fell, it fell on four gigantic taloned feet. It raised its spiny head and waved its monstrous tail. Its open jaws roared defiance at the tiger.

It reared up. It slashed, and its talons added stripes of blood to the tiger's hide. It bit, and rivers of blood stained the earth. Vainly the tiger clawed at its impenetrable scales. It had no chance. In moments it was struck down, with a thud to shake the world. Everything was riven apart, and with it Hao Sen.

For an instant he saw the rival armies, the gory ground, the dead and dying, and—

And it was over and he was Howson, not Hao Sen, and he was full of a nameless terror because of the way he had won.

*H*e stood at the end of the bed where they had put Choong to recover, waiting for him to wake up. Meantime, he had no refuge from his thoughts.

I think that Miss Moreno knew; at any rate, she left so quickly, before I'd slept off my exhaustion. . . . And Pan knows, but I can trust him after the times we've worked together.

Pandit Singh, of course, had no inkling of the terrible truth which had come to Howson. He was going around radiating paternal pride, and all the UN people—Lockspeiser and Ho and everybody—were feeling apologetic for doubting him in the first place, and Howson felt mainly a dull ache.

His triumph had been a sham. The whole business had been set up like tenpins for him, and he had been given an unlimited number of balls.

And here was Choong, who had treated him like a plaything, who was happily married and physically whole, and the world was so grossly unjust he didn't know how long he could stand it.

Choong stirred, and it was as though a gigantic light had been switched on in the room; everything stood out in bright three-dimensional forms compared to which there had been gray dusk. That was his perception waking up. Only another telepathist would have realized there was a difference.

His eyes opened. There was a moment of blankness. Then:

I seem to know you . . . ?

"Yes, you know me. Gerald Howson." Deliberately he

used words; he was shutting down every batten he could over his raging mind. "You've made a fool of me, haven't you? Well, I want to know why!"

There was another blank moment, during which Choong ordered his thoughts with a swiftness which impressed Howson despite his preconceived anger.

"So you handled my . . . ah . . . case," Choong said, and gave a wry smile. "I'm sorry. I wouldn't have thought it necessary to bother you, of all people. A comparative novice should have been assigned to me. I thought I'd made it pretty clear that I wasn't on the run, and would be willing to be brought back."

Howson almost choked before he could reply; when he did, it was with such a blaze of fury that he used projection instead of words.

How can you be so casually selfish? Don't you care about the worry and trouble you've caused? Don't you care about the annoyance to me personally? What about the time I wasted—time I could have given to somebody in real need?

Choong cried out and put his hand to his head. The door of the room slammed back and a nurse looked in to ask what was wrong. Recovering, Choong waved her away, and with a suspicious glance at Howson she complied.

"You have some power on you!" Choong said. "Do you mind sticking to speech? My mind feels rather . . . ah . . . bruised from your earlier shock tactics."

Howson remained sullenly mute.

"Did it honestly not occur to you that I wouldn't resist?" Choong pursued. "Yes, I see it was so, right up till the last moment! I find that astonishing, if you'll forgive my saying so. You must have jumped to the conclusion that the only reason a telepathist could wish to set up a catapathic grouping was to escape; it never struck you that I might simply wish to exercise my talent for its own rewarding sake!"

"Don't gloat," Howson muttered. "I know I could never have dragged you back if you hadn't cooperated."

"No, I think you're missing the point." Choong activated the headboard of the bed and got himself into a more comfortable position from which to look at Howson. "Damn it, Howson, you wouldn't blame a man with physical gifts for enjoying himself at sports. Yet it seems to me that you have a block against the idea that telepathy can be used for pleasure. Why? You have a fabulous talent! And I'm by no means sure you wouldn't have got me back even if I had resisted; the sudden final inspiration was brilliant, and took me absolutely by surprise. Don't you ever get any fun out of your gift? For instance, my wife and I usually link up before we go to sleep; I dream much more vividly than she does, and I like her to share my dreams."

"I'm not married," Howson said in a tight voice. Choong flashed an impolite glance into his mind, briefly vulnerable from the strength of his emotion. When he spoke again, it was with a change of manner.

"I'm sorry. That was tactless of me. But—"

"I . . ." Howson felt a stir of puzzlement. Why should he need to justify himself suddenly to this man who had put him to such trouble? But he did. Haltingly, he went on, "I've done that sort of thing. With a deaf-and-dumb girl I knew."

"Well, then! And you must enjoy your work to some extent. If for no other reason than that it makes a change to be a tough, resilient character capable of great physical effort."

"I . . . yes, I do. I'm sometimes afraid of taking longer than necessary over a cure so that I can escape my limitations." Howson licked his lips.

"That sounds dangerous," Choong said judiciously. "My belief is that if you allowed yourself to derive more pleasure from your talent, you wouldn't be tempted to . . . ah . . . borrow other people's fantasies."

"What are you suggesting?" Howson demanded. "That I set up a catapathic grouping myself? How could I dare to? Even if I accepted your casual attitude toward them!" *Vargas, and dust on his eyelids* . . . "I wouldn't have much incentive to come back to reality, would I? And whom could I trust to bring me back? I've demolished all the tricks and weak points. On top of that, if someone *did* manage to fetch me back, what would happen to my confidence in my own ability?"

The nurse opened the door again. "Dr. Howson! Message from Dr. van Osterbeck: you're not to undo your work by making Dr. Choong overtired!"

Howson made an empty gesture and turned to limp away. Behind him Choong spoke up one final time.

"'Just because an escape which suits me or someone else doesn't suit you, Howson, doesn't mean there isn't one for you. You're a unique individual. Find your own way. There's bound to be one!"

Howson wasn't quite sure whether Choong had physically spoken those last few words, or eased them telepathically into his mind with the practiced skill of a first-class psychiatrist implanting a suggestion in a patient. In a patient . . . that was funny! A few days before, Howson had been the doctor in charge; a moment had seen the roles reversed.

Except that Choong had never actually been the patient Howson had believed him to be.

He had already ordered his personal attendant to pack his bags. Now, outside Pandit Singh's office, he found himself hesitating. Would he be able to make clear what he felt, what he wanted? Did he in fact know himself what he wanted?

He steeled himself and went in. Anything, surely, would be better than his present dilemma!

Singh didn't raise his head from the mound of papers before him, merely waved at a chair. "Sit down, Gerry; won't keep you a moment. Ah . . . there!" He scrawled a hasty signature on the topmost document and threw it into the out tray.

Leaning back, he said, "I agree, Gerry. You need a vacation."

Not for the first time, not for the hundredth, Howson found he was wondering whether Singh had embryo telepathic faculties himself. Flushing, he said, "What . . . ?"

"Oh, Gerry, for pity's sake!" Singh rumbled a cheerful laugh. "I've been told about your bags being packed. When I heard, I calculated that it was six years since you last had a rest. It's partly my fault: I've grown accustomed to leaning on you. But you haven't seemed nearly as pleased as you should be with your success in Choong's case, and my deduction is that you want a vacation. I'm glad you agree with me."

Howson was silent for a long moment. Then he said, "Pan, I'm afraid you're wrong."

"You're not . . . ?" The suspicion that Howson was planning a permanent departure leaped up in Singh's appalled mind.

"Ohhhh!" In exasperation Howson cancelled the mistaken assumption with a telepathic correction, and went on aloud. "The Choong case wasn't a success for me, Pan. He wanted to be brought back. If he hadn't cooperated—or at least not resisted with any seriousness—I'd have been beaten."

"Gerry, I don't understand!"

"No? Nor did I, at first," Howson agreed bitterly. "And Pak wouldn't have told you, I guess, because I warned him not to unless I had a chance to get used to the idea. Listen! All the telepathists I've previously routed out of their dreams were the inadequate personalities we assumed them to be, broken by the harshness of the world. Them I can tackle. Choong in full command of his faculties, in a world of his own devising and operating at his own whim, could have brushed me off like an annoying fly.

"He didn't. He had the sense to see that he was going to have to help whoever came after him, as a precaution against enjoying his absolute power too greatly. So he followed sets of easily deducible rules. In particular, when he incorporated magic into his private universe, he employed the basic James Frazer rules of like-to-like and part-to-whole. I took him by surprise when I suddenly realized this during the crucial encounter, and . . . well, never mind the details. Just say that's the only thing I'm pleased with, and it doesn't satisfy me because it was a lucky inspiration, not the result of planning and foresight.

"Pan, he's punctured my confidence! I've had to admit something I've hidden for years from you, even from myself. I'm *jealous* of people who can escape into fugue! Why not? Look at me! And I'm scared because I'm jealous. There's no one I know of who could come and get *me* back out of fantasy! Unless I do something to help myself, I'm apt to go into some patient's universe and find it so much to my liking I don't want to come back. I haven't the guts to go into it the way Choong did. But I might well not have the guts to cut short a . . . a trip to some especially attractive fantasy."

Singh was staring down at the top of his desk. He said, "Do I take it that you have in mind something you can do to help yourself?"

"I . . . I'm not sure." Sweat was prickly on Howson's face and hands now. "All I've decided so far is that I'm going away for a while. Alone. Not the way I used to go when I first came here, with someone to watch over me in case I cut myself or children mocked me, but alone. Maybe I can't go rock-climbing in the Caucasus; maybe I can't go surfing at Bondi Beach. But . . . damn it, Pan, I looked after myself, more or less, for twenty years before I was discovered and brought in. If I can relearn to do that much, I may be on the track of an answer to my problems."

"I see." Singh turned a pen over between his short, capable fingers. "You're not going to do anything as stupid as throwing away your prothrombin, I take it?"

"Hardly! Independence has limits. But dependence has, too, I want to set some for myself, that's all."

"So what do you propose to do now?"

"Send for a cab, go to the airport, and take a plane somewhere. I'll be back in—oh—a couple of months, I guess. You'll see I get money?"

"Of course."

"Well, then . . ." Howson felt at a loss. "Well, that seems to be all, doesn't it?"

"I imagine so." Singh rose and came around the desk, holding out his hand. "Good luck, Gerry. I hope you find what you want for yourself."

Abruptly he wasn't looking at Howson any longer. He was facing an olive-skinned man with a square black beard, standing taller than himself, wearing a peculiar barbaric costume mostly of leather studded with tarnished brass. A huge sword dangled from his belt. He was muscular, good-looking; he radiated health and contentment.

The stranger changed; melted; shrank until he was

barely five feet tall and beardless and slightly deformed—
until he was, in fact, Gerald Howson.

"That's what I want," said Howson in a thin voice.
"That's not what will be any good to me, though. Good-
bye, Pan. And thank you."

xxi

A t the airport he inquired about flights to the city
where he had been born, and was almost shocked
to recollect that it had once been his home.

Home! How long since he last thought of it as such? For
years "home" had meant his apartment in the therapy
center, with everything tailored to his special needs—even
the sanitary fittings in the adjacent bathroom—so that
the chair he kept for visitors, of normal size, seemed
intrusive.

Yet some part of him had never caught up with that
shift of perspective. Maybe this trip was really intended
to look for what he had left behind.

Would people remember and recognize him? He
hadn't changed much, but he was well-dressed instead of
shabby, well-fed instead of pinched and scrawny—enough
change, maybe, to make people pucker their foreheads
in search of a half-vanished memory.

A curious heady excitement began to take hold of him
as his cab rolled through familiar streets toward the district where most of his childhood had been spent. On impulse, he told the hackie to stop and let him out. He
had checked most of his bags at the airport, keeping only
a light valise which he could handle easily, and he wanted
to take this stage of the journey slowly, on foot, to let the
impact of old associations seep into his mind.

The first major fact to register on him was that his
old home had gone.

He stood on a street corner and looked at the towering stack of low-priced apartments which had taken the place of the plaster-peeling rabbit warren of a tenement he had known. The same kind of street gangs chased past him; the same wheezing old cars rolled by; the same crowded buses clanged and burped down the street. But the building wasn't there.

An unexpected pang of nostalgia touched him. He had never imagined he could regret the disappearance of a place which had brought him so little of pleasure to cherish. He changed hands on his valise and limped on. As he went, he found people staring at him; a small boy bravely threw a dirty word at him and dissolved into laughter. He knew, now, why such things were done, and felt no resentment.

A block or two north, he remembered, was a bar and grill where he had done odd jobs during his mother's illness. The way to it would take him past the school he had attended. He turned northward, making mental comparisons as he went.

The atmosphere was different from what he recollected. He had a sense of something like tranquillity, contrasting with the frenzied modernity of Ulan Bator with its cosmopolitan influx of strangers. Maybe this was the ultimate effect of the crisis in whose shadow he had been born. The closest he could come to summing it up in a single word was "chastened." But there was no regret apparent.

He found himself rather liking the sensation, and wishing he had been back earlier.

The bar and grill had changed in layout and decor, but it was still there. It seemed more prosperous than in the old days. There were high stools at the counter, but he went to a table, earning a grimace from the lounging counterman; he found it much too difficult to perch on a stool.

"What'll it be?" the counterman called.

He was hungry after his journey, Howson found. "Small portion of steak and French fries, and a can of beer," he responded.

While he was waiting for the food to come from the kitchen, the counterman eyed his visitor curiously. It was plain why, but Howson waited until he raised the question openly.

"Here y'are, shorty," the young man said in a friendly enough manner, setting the plate and glass on Howson's table. "Hey . . . I think I seen you around here some place, a long time back! Didn't I?"

He would have been about twelve when Howson left, probably; it was quite possible he remembered. "You might have," Howson agreed cautiously. "Does Charlie Birberger still run this place?"

"Mm-hm. You a friend of his?"

"I used to be." Howson hesitated. "If he's in, maybe he'd come and have a word with me."

"I'll ask," said the counterman obligingly.

There was an exchange of shouts; then Birberger himself, older, fatter, but otherwise unchanged, came blinking into the bar. He caught sight of Howson and stopped dead, his mind a kaleidoscope of astonishment.

He recovered quickly, and waddled across the floor with a jovial air. "By God! Sarah Howson's boy! Well, I never expected to see you in this place again after all we heard about you! Making out pretty well, hey?"

"Pretty well," Howson said. "Won't you sit down?"

"Uh? Oh, sure!" Birberger fumbled a chair away from the table and entrusted his bulk to it gingerly. He put both elbows on the table, leaning forward. "We see about you in the papers sometimes, y'know! Must be wonderful work you're doing. Must admit, I never expected you to wind up where you are! Uh . . . been a pretty long time since you were here, hey? Ten years!"

"Eleven," said Howson quietly.

"Long as that? Well, well!" Birberger rambled on. There was a faint quaver in his rotund voice, and Howson was suddenly struck by a strange realization: *Damn it, the man's scared!*

"Uh . . . any special reason for coming back?" Birberger probed clumsily. "Or just looking up the old place?"

"Looking up old friends, more," Howson corrected. He took a sip of his beer. "You're the first I've met since I flew in an hour or two back."

"Well, it's good of you to count me as an old friend,"

Birberger said, brightening. "Y'know, I often think of the days when I useta let you help out in here. I remember you had quite an appetite for a—" He might have been going to say "runt," but caught himself and finished with a change of mental gears: "Uh—young fella!"

He sat back. "Y'know, I like to think maybe I managed to give you a helping hand now and again. With your mother sick, and all . . ."

Howson could see the rose-colored filters going up in his memory. He hid a smile. Charlie Birberger had been an irritable, hard-to-get-on-with employer, given to bawling out his assistants mercilessly—especially Gerry Howson.

Well, no matter. He nodded as though in agreement, and Birberger's original disquiet faded still further.

"Hey, tell you something!" the fat man said. "I still have all the cuttings from the papers about how they found you. I guess I could dig them out and show you. Hang on!"

He hoisted himself to his feet and disappeared into the back rooms. In a few minutes he returned with a dusty album, which he made ineffectual attempts to blow clean as he sat down again.

"There!" he said, opening it and turning it so that Howson could read the yellow cuttings it contained.

Howson laid down his knife and fork and leafed through the album curiously. He hadn't realized that the discovery of a telepathist had created such a furor in the city. Here were front-page items from all the leading local papers, some of them with pictures of Danny Waldemar and other UN personnel.

He had come to the last page and was about to hand the book back with a word of thanks, when he hesitated. The final item seemed to be completely irrelevant; it was a single paragraph reporting the marriage of Miss Mary Hall and Mr. Stephen Williams, and the date was about two years after his departure.

"This one," he said, putting a finger on it. "Is it connected with the rest?"

Birberger craned to study it. He frowned. "Now, what in—? If it's there, sure as hell there's a reason. Must have something to do with— Good *God,* I remember!" He stared in astonishment at Howson. "Don't you know the name? I'd have thought you of all people . . . !"

Blankly, Howson returned the gaze. And then he had it.

He shut his eyes; the impact was almost physical. In a husky tone he said, "No . . . no, I never knew her name. She was deaf and dumb, you see, so she couldn't tell me. And after she got her speech and hearing she only came to see me a few times."

"She never wrote you?" Birberger was turning back the leaves of the album. "After all you did for her, too? I'm really surprised. Yes, here we are: 'A plane from Ulan Bator today brought in eighteen-year-old Mary Hall, the deaf-and-dumb girl who befriended novice telepathist Gerry Howson. She told reporters at the city airport that the operation to give her artificial speech and hearing was completely successful, and now all she wanted was the chance to lead a quiet, normal life.' Look!"

At first glance he must have missed it because he wanted to, Howson told himself. For the newspaper photo wasn't a bad one. There she was, standing at the door of the plane: smartly dressed, true, and wearing make-up and with her hair properly styled, but recognizably the girl he had known.

"Is there any chance of finding out where she's living?" He had uttered the question unplanned, but realized its inevitability while Birberger was still rubbing his chin and considering the problem.

"I'll get the city directory!" he said, rather too eagerly, as though anxious to get Howson on his way.

There were several dozen Williamses, but only one Stephen Williams. Howson studied the address.

"West Walnut," he said. "Where's that?"

"New district since your time, I believe. Big development outside town. A Number Nineteen bus goes direct." Birberger was hardly making any attempt to disguise his desire to see the back of his visitor now.

So Howson, dispirited, accommodated him, paying for his food and beer and gathering up his valise. Birberger stumped to the door with him and insisted on shaking his hand, treating it with care as if touching something rare and fragile. But his invitation to come back as soon as possible rang thin.

On impulse Howson asked him, "Say, Mr. Birberger! What's your picture of the kind of work I do nowadays?"

Startled, the fat man improvised. "Why, you—you sort of look into crazy people's minds and tell what's wrong with them. And straighten them out. Don't you?"

"That's right," Howson said a little unkindly. "Don't worry, though—I'm not looking into your mind. After all, you're not crazy, are you?"

The seeds of the most peculiar kind of doubt were germinating in Birberger's mind as Howson limped down the street toward the stop for a Nineteen bus.

Odd, people's different reactions to telepathists. . .

Howson contemplated them as he sat in the single seat near the driver up front in the bus. He hadn't examined that problem for years; at the WHO therapy center he was in isolation from it, because telepathists had become a completely accepted part of the regular staff.

Occasionally, though not as often as he would have liked, trainees came in, and he assisted with their development. Each was unique, and consequently each responded differently to knowledge of his talent. Some were like children with a new-found toy; others were like members of a family in Nazi Germany, who had just discovered that they had Jewish blood and were desperately pretending it made no difference.

It was getting easier to accept the gift, granted. The years of carefully devised propaganda had had some effect. But telepathists were so few they barely even constituted a minority group, and that, rather than conditioning of the public, had been their salvation—at least in Howson's view. A tiny fraction of the population had actually met someone with the power; consequently, though most people had opinions ("I don't doubt they do wonderful work, but I wouldn't like someone poking around in *my* mind— I mean, it's the ultimate invasion of privacy!"), few had formed lasting attitudes.

"West Walnut, pal!" the driver called to him, slowing the bus. He was trying to control his prejudice reactions at Howson's appearance, and for that Howson gave him a

projective wave of warm gratitude. It lighted the man's
mind like a gaudy show of fireworks, and he was whistling
a cheerful tune as he drove away.

Howson gave a bitter chuckle. If it were always that
easy, things would be fine!

xxii

The new development was clean, airy, spacious, with
small houses set among bright green lawns. Children
on their way home from school ran and laughed along
the paths. He thought achingly of the close, ugly streets of
his own childhood, and repressed absurd envy. Briskening
his pace as much as possible, he followed signs toward the
Williams home.

Yes, there was the name on the mailbox: S. WILLIAMS.
He reached up and pressed the bell.

After a while the door was cautiously opened on a se-
curity chain, and a girl of about seven looked through the
gap. "'What do you want?" she said timidly.

"Is Mrs. Williams in?"

"Mummy isn't home," the girl said in her most grown-up
and authoritative voice. "I'm dreadfully sorry."

"Will she be back soon? I'm an old friend of hers, and I
want to—"

"What is it, Jill?" a boy's voice inquired from out of
sight.

"There's a man here who wants to see Mummy," the
girl explained, and a clatter of shoes announced her
brother's descent of the stairs. In a moment another pair
of eyes was peering at the visitor. The boy was startled at
Howson's appearance, and failed to conceal the fact, but
he had obviously been trained to be polite, and opened
the door with an invitation to come in and wait.

"Mummy's gone to see Mrs. Olling next door," he said. "She won't be long."

Howson thanked him and limped into the lounge. Behind him he heard an argument going on in whispers—Jill complaining that they oughtn't to have let a stranger into the house, and her brother countering scornfully that Howson was no bigger than himself, so how could he be dangerous?

Shyly, the children followed him into the lounge and sat down on a sofa opposite the chair he had taken, at a loss for anything to say. Howson had not had anything to do with children for many years; he felt almost equally tongue-tied.

"Maybe your mother has told you about me," he ventured. "I'm called Gerry—Gerry Howson. I used to know your mother when she was—uh—before she met your daddy. You're Jill, aren't you? And . . . ?"

"I'm Bobby," said the boy. "Er . . . do you live near here, Mr. Howson?"

"No, I live at Ulan Bator. I'm a doctor at the big hospital there."

"A doctor!" This began to thaw Jill's shyness. She leaned forward excitedly. "Ooh! I'm going to be a nurse when I grow up."

"How about you, Bobby? Do you want to be a doctor?"

"No, I don't," said the boy rather slightingly. "I want to be a Mars pilot or a submarine captain." Then he relented, and with a gravity exactly imitated from some stiff-mannered adult, he added, "I'm sure a doctor's work is very interesting, though."

"Mr. Howson," said Jill with a puzzled expression. "If you're a doctor, why have you got a bad leg? Can't you have it fixed?"

"Jill!" exclaimed Bobby, horrified. "You *know* you shouldn't say things like that to people!"

He *was* being grown-up, thought Howson with amusement. "I don't mind," he said. "No, Jill, I can't have it fixed. I was born like it, and now there's nothing that can be done. Besides, I'm not that kind of doctor. "I . . ." He recollected Birberger's halting, naïve description of his work, and finished, "I look into sick people's minds and tell what's wrong with them."

Bobby's adult manners vanished in a wave of surprise. "You mean you're a *crazy* doctor?"

"Well, now!" Howson countered with a hint of a smile. "I don't think 'crazy' is a very nice word. The people who come to my hospital are pretty much the same as anybody; they just need help because life has got too complicated for them."

They didn't contest the statement, but their skepticism was apparent. Howson sighed. "How would you like me to tell you a story about my work?" he suggested. "I used to tell stories to your mother, and she enjoyed it."

"Depends on the story," said Bobby cautiously. Jill had been sitting in wide-eyed wonder since Howson's revelation that he was a "crazy doctor." Now she spoke up in support of her brother.

"I don't think we'd like a story about crazy people," she said doubtfully.

"It's very exciting," Howson promised quietly. "Much more exciting than being a spaceman or a submarine captain, really. I have a wonderful job." He found time to ask himself when he had last realized how completely he meant that declaration, before he went on.

"Suppose I tell you about this person who came to my hospital. . . ."

The technique came back to him as though he had used it yesterday, instead of eleven years before. Gently he projected the hint that the children should shut their eyes, just as he had done long ago for the deaf-and-dumb girl whose mind was closed to anything but bright plain images and rich sensory impressions.

First . . . A hospital ward: efficiency, confidence, kindliness. Pretty nurses—Jill could be one of them for an instant, calming a patient whose face reflected gratitude.

Now . . . A glance inside the patient's mind. Nightmare: but not a child's nightmare, which would have been too terrifying for them. An adult nightmare, rather—too complex for them to recognize more than its superficial nature.

And then . . . Sharp, well-defined images: the patient running through the corridors of his own mind pursued by monsters from his subconscious; running for help and finding none until the presence of the doctor suggested reassurance and comfort. Then the harrying horrors paused in their chase; arming themselves with weapons which they could create merely by thinking, patient and doctor together cowed the things, drove them back, cornered them —and they were not.

It was a compound of half a dozen cases he had handled as a novice, simple, vigorous and exciting without being too fearful. When he had done, Howson broke the link and suggested that they open their eyes again.

"Goodness!" said Bobby with considerable new respect. "I didn't know it was like that at all!"

Jill was about to confirm his reaction when she glanced through the open door into the hallway and bounced to her feet. "There's Mummy!" she exclaimed. "Mummy, here's somebody to see you. He's been telling us such an exciting story, like the ones he used to tell you!"

Mary Williams pushed the door fully open and looked at Howson. Her face—rather coarse, as he remembered it, but showing more personality and cleverly made up— set in a frozen stare. Through lips which barely opened, she said, "That was nice of him. Now you run along so I can talk to Mr. Howson on my own."

Obediently the children started for the door. "Will you tell us some more stories sometime, please?" Jill threw over her shoulder as she went out.

"If you like," Howson promised, smiling, and when they had gone, added to Mary, "Two fine children you have there!"

She ignored the remark. With her face still icy cold and empty, she said, "Well, Gerry? So you've come back to plague me, have you?"

Howson waited in blank astonishment for a few seconds. When she did not amplify this amazing statement, he got to his feet. "I came to find out how you were getting on," he snapped. "If you call it plaguing you, I'll go. Right now!"

He picked up his valise, half-expecting her to open the door and say it was good riddance. Instead, she burst into tears.

"Mary!" he exclaimed, and realized and added aloud in the same moment: "Why, that's the first time I've ever called you by name! And we knew each other pretty well, didn't we?"

She mastered her sobs, and gestured for him to sit down again. "I'm sorry," she said weakly. It was amazing how completely she had learned to use her artificial vocal cords; unless one looked carefully for the scar on her throat, it was impossible to detect they had been inserted by the hand of man. "It just took me by surprise, I guess. It . . . it's nice of you to call, Gerry."

"But what did you mean when you said I'd come to plague you?"

"Isn't it obvious?" She moved to the place where Jill had been sitting, and waved vaguely at her surroundings —the room, the house, the whole suburb. "Now that you have come, what have you found? An ordinary housewife with a couple of ordinary kids and a decent enough guy for a husband. You can find a million people like me wherever you go. Only . . ."

She dabbed her eyes with a handkerchief and sat up, crossing her legs. "Only seeing you reminded me of what I was going to be. . . . That was why I stopped coming to see you."

"I think I understand," Howson said faintly. A cold weight was settling in the pit of his stomach. "But I never suspected there was anything wrong. You seemed so happy!"

"Oh, I guess I didn't really suspect it myself." She stared past him at the plain pastel walls. "It was after I came home that I realized. You remember how—in the stories you used to tell me—I was always beautiful and sought after, and I could hear and talk like anyone else." She gave a harsh laugh.

"Well, the only part that came true was the 'like anyone else'! I thought I'd got over it—until I came through the door and saw you sitting there. And it reminded me that instead of being the . . . the princess in the fairy tale, I'm plain Mary Williams the West Walnut housewife, and I shall never be anything else."

There was silence for a moment. Howson could think of nothing to say.

"And of course I've been so jealous of you," she went on in a level tone. "While I had to drop back into this anonymous existence, you became important and famous. . . ."

"I suppose you wouldn't believe me," said Howson meditatively, "if I were to tell you that sometimes I feel I'd give up fame, importance, everything, for the privilege of looking other men straight in the eye and walking down the street without a limp."

In an odd voice she said, "Yes, Gerry, I think I do believe you. I heard they hadn't been able to do anything—about your leg, I mean. And the rest of it. I'm sorry."

A thought struck her, and she stiffened. "Gerry, you haven't really been telling Jill and Bobby the same kind of stories you told me? I'd never forgive you if you cursed them with the same kind of discontent."

"I've learned a lot in eleven years," Howson said bitterly. "You needn't worry. I just told them about my work at Ulan Bator, and Jill says she wants to be a nurse anyway. I don't think it will leave them discontented."

"It left me that way," Mary mused. "I remember the stories you told me much more vividly than I remember the dreadful place where we were living. The stories are more . . . more definite. While the real world has faded into a blur of gray."

Howson had not yet replied when there were steps in the hall, and the sound of the children running. A man's voice was heard greeting them affectionately.

"There's Steve," said Mary dispiritedly. "I wish—"

Howson didn't hear what she wished, for at that moment Williams entered the room and stopped in surprise at seeing Howson there. "Uh—good afternoon!" he said blankly, his eyes asking furious questions of his wife.

"Steve, this is—I guess I should call you 'doctor,' shouldn't I, Gerry?—Dr. Gerry Howson, from Ulan Bator. He used to be a friend of mine before I met you."

Williams signally failed to mask the fact that he thought his wife's choice of friends must have been peculiar, but he offered his hand and Howson rose to take it.

"Gerry's a psychiatrist," Mary explained further, and Howson shook his head, wondering why she hadn't told her husband about him.

"Not exactly. I'm actually a curative telepathist on the

staff of the therapy center there—the Asian headquarters of WHO."

"A telepathist!" The information shook Williams severely. "Well, how—uh—interesting! I never met one of you people before." *And never particularly wanted to,* his mind glossed silently.

There was a pause. Mary tried to fill it by saying in a bright voice, "You'll stay for supper with us, Gerry, I hope?" But behind the words he could read desperate anxiety: *Please say no: I never told him about you and I don't think I could bear to have you reminding me, reminding me....*

Howson made great play of looking at his watch. "I'd love to," he lied. "But I haven't got too much time and I want to look up a good many old acquaintances. I'd better say no."

He collected his valise and took his leave. On the doorstep he looked back at Mary.

"Apologize to the children for my not being able to stay and tell them another story, won't you?" he said. "And . . . try not to hate me."

"I promise," said Mary with a wan smile.

"And try not to pity me, either!" he finished savagely, turning his back. He wished he could have stormed down the path from the house, instead of hobbling like a rather ridiculous jointed doll.

xxiii

*F*or many years the hope had endured in his mind: that the deaf-and-dumb girl who had been kind to him had not suffered lastingly because of him. He had believed that there if anywhere he had managed ultimately to ensure a person's happiness.

He had avoided questioning the assumption. Why? Because he subconsciously realized the truth?

The encounter with her had jolted his personality to its foundations. For a while, as he limped toward the high-way fringing the West Walnut development, he was inclined to abandon his trip at once, unwilling to face any more such revelations. But this was exactly what he must *not* do; no matter how unique his talent made him, he remained a human being, and he had come hunting for the completion of that humanity.

He sighed, put his valise down on the sidewalk and looked both ways along the street. A cab was turning around after dropping a dark-suited man, home from work. He waved at the driver, wondering where he should ask to be taken now.

The vehicle went on by. In sudden anger Howson made as if to project a deafening mental shout after it, but at the last moment he realized the driver had mistaken him for a kid waving a greeting because of his small size, and contented himself with suggesting that the man think again.

The cab braked, reversed, pulled up to where he stood. The hackie, a thick-set man with humorous eyes, took in Howson's appearance, considered it, shrugged. He said, "Sorry, pal—dreaming, I guess. I lose more fares . . Where to, anyway?"

"Grand Avenue," Howson said briefly, and scrambled in.

Now the name was ridiculous. The process of disintegration which had begun at the time of Howson's birth and was well under way when he left for Ulan Bator had gone nearly to completion. A stretch of four blocks at the north end of the avenue was being demolished and laid out as a city housing project; beyond, as though disheartened by the threat of extinction, the stores had closed their eyes behind lids of crude bright posters: EVERYTHING MUST GO! CLEARANCE SALE! LEASE UP, BARGAIN TIME NOW!

An evening wind pushed balls of paper and clouds of dust down the unswept gutters, and the few people about walked with an air of gloom.

There was the movie theater where he had conceived his first and disastrous attempt at importance, still struggling on, but grimy and neglected. And beyond it, something entirely new: a handsome, clean, tall block with discreet bronze lettering on the marble pillars of its main door. Frowning, Howson considered what they said.

CENTRAL UNIVERSITY—FACULTY OF PURE AND APPLIED SCIENCE.

"Driver!" he called. "Take it slow along here, will you?"

Complying with a dab on his brakes, the driver glanced over his shoulder. "Makes a difference, doesn't it?" he commented. "That's the Drake Gift, that place. Whole big piece of land given to the university a few years back. Going to have room for a thousand students when they're through—classrooms, offices, dormitories!"

Well, that was an improvement, no denying. But once more Howson felt the unaccountable stab of nostalgia at the disappearance of a place he had never thought he would want to see again.

"Is it already in use?" he asked.

"Oh sure—since last fall. They put the students into rooms all around this district so they needn't wait till the dormitories are ready."

Way, way back young Gerry Howson had had visions of going to college, then on to some academic career. . . . He stifled the memory with an effort. Even if he had got further than he had done toward his goal, his gift would have developed sooner or later and everything else would have had to take second place anyway. He wouldn't have got where he was by the same route, but he would have been forced here eventually.

"Is there still a bar along here on the right?" he asked. "The one that used to be run by a guy called Horace Hampton?"

"The Snake?" The driver twisted his head clear around at that. "You must have been away a long time, pal! I recall The Snake, but only just! Why—uh—ten years back, I guess, some teeps came in from the UN and went through the big rackets and cleared 'em out. The Snake got five years with compulsory rehabilitation for accessory to murder, and last I heard he was going to join some UN outfit and make good."

Teeps—TP's—telepathists. Howson nodded. He didn't remember hearing the nickname before, which surprised him; it was so obvious. As for the news about Snake

Hampton, it was less strange that he shouldn't have known that. This was, after all, a city that the new world was passing by. A minor law-enforcement action was petty compared to the big jobs the—the *teeps* had undertaken here.

"But his bar's still going," the driver said. "Just coming into sight ahead, there. I don't know who runs it now."

"There's a hotel the other side of it," Howson said. "Drop me there."

Having checked in at the hotel and arranged for the rest of his bags to be sent down from the airport, he ate a solitary meal and reflected on what he had found out so far. He felt despondent. Why should he have expected to be able to come back to where he had left off eleven years ago? It seemed an arrogant assumption, and annoyed him.

He was a stranger now. He'd have to accept that.

After his meal he left the hotel and went along the street to what had been Hampton's bar. It was shabbier, more dimly lighted than he remembered, its mirrors flyspecked, its floor worn by many feet. Were the rooms in back as they had been—the blue room where he had spent those anxious hours with Lots, for example? Did it matter? He had made up his mind not to look for things as they had been, but as they were now. He moved to a corner table at the back of the bar, ordered a beer, and sat miserably contemplating it.

The image of Mary's face kept getting between him and the world around him. It was going to take a long time to adjust to what she had confessed to him. "Why," Hugh Choong had asked him, in effect, "do you feel guilty about using your ability for your own enjoyment?"

And he might have answered, "Because when I did I was repaid with the subconscious knowledge that I had created suffering."

Poor Mary . . . Poor fairy-tale princess!

Other things were growing clear in his mind, too. Charlie Birberger had been eager to convince himself that he had given Howson a helping hand; well, how much of Howson's own insistence on staying the year around at the Ulan Bator hospital was due to a desire to see as many patients as possible feel indebted to him? Was he in fact being influenced by the urge to secure their admiration and gratitude, as he had sought Mary's admiration and gratitude eleven years before?

He broke off the train of thought in annoyance. Self-analysis like this could go on indefinitely and never get anywhere. He had indisputably done a hell of a lot of good work, and he would do more—provided only that he could restore his confidence in himself. So far he had managed to destroy some self-defensive illusions; granted, if they were illusions they were fragile anyway, but they had helped to sustain him in the past, so he was making his situation worse instead of better.

Where to from here? What next?

He raised his beer and sipped it, thinking about the first time he had come in here and the exchange he had had with Lots about the reason for his not drinking. He had learned from the minds of well-adjusted colleagues why people did like to drink, and stopped there, with the vicarious ability to copy them. He had also seen why some of his patients drank to excess, and preferred not to be taken in by the same fallacy.

Setting the glass down, he became aware of raised voices at the table in the corner opposite his own. A group of two young men—untidily dressed and about two days unshaven—and a plain girl with fair hair in a rather shapeless dress were involved in heated argument. At least, one man and the girl were; the other man seemed to be listening with amusement.

"But don't you *see?*" thundered the girl, slamming her open palm on the table so that the trio's glasses jumped. "You're ignoring the lessons of the whole of the past century in order to rehash things which have been done twenty times over better than *you'll* ever manage to do them!"

"You must be blind, deaf, dumb and moronic to say a thing like that!" blazed back her opponent. "One of your most damnable faults, and you've got plenty, is making wild and empty generalizations! Anyone with a grain of intelligence—"

"Excuse me, you two," said the mildly amused young man. "I'll come back when it's less noisy around here."

"Good riddance!" snapped the girl as he picked up his drink and crossed the floor to Howson's table. Howson bridled instinctively, but the stranger betrayed no reaction to his appearance.

"Mind if I sit here for a bit? I won't be able to get a word in edgewise until they calm down, and since neither of them really knows what they're talking about . . . Cigarette?"

Howson was on the point of refusing—smoking was discouraged at the therapy center, even with carcinogen-free tobacco available now—when it occurred to him that the young man was being extremely courteous. He had no means of knowing that Howson was more than his vacuous face suggested, yet had addressed him with perfect aplomb.

He accepted the cigarette with a word of thanks.

"What's it all about, anyway?" he ventured as he bent to receive a light.

"Charma," said the other around his cigarette, "insists that Jay is doing incompetent and unsatisfactory work. She's right. She is, however, totally wrong in maintaining that he's merely repeating something that's been done hundreds of times. He does have a fairly original idea; he simply isn't good enough to cope with it properly. He thinks he is. So . . . they disagree."

"Does this happen a lot?"

"It goes on all the blasted time!" said the young man in a ponderously aggrieved tone.

"And what sort of work?"

"Oh, it's a bit hard to define. I guess you might call his things liquid mobiles. Charma refers to them as wet fireworks, and though I suppose you could argue that she has something there, it doesn't exactly delight Jay. Main trouble is, he ought to be a chemist and hydrodynamicist as well as a guy with an eye for a lighting effect, and he isn't, so he can't exploit the very genuine possibilities of his technique."

About twenty-two or three, Howson judged as he looked at his new acquaintance. He was of medium height, plumply good-looking, with untidy black hair and heavy glasses. He wore a faded shirt open at the neck, dark trousers with light stains on the knees, and open sandals.

An enormous watch caught the light on his wrist. A sheaf of pens and pencils was clipped in his shirt pocket.

"You're students?" suggested Howson, recollecting the nearness of the new university building.

"No more, no more. We got a wee bit dissatisfied with academic standards a while back, and since the academic standard-bearers were likewise less than pleased with us, we agreed to stop bothering each other. Another drink?"

"No, let me," said Howson, and signaled a waiter. He paid with the topmost of a bundle of bills that made his companion purse his mouth in parodied awe.

"It always gives me pleasure to accept a drink from the rich," he said solemnly. "It means I'm doing my humble bit toward the redistribution of capital."

"Set 'em up for those two as well," Howson told the waiter, indicating Jay and Charma. "Ah . . . what's your particular line, by the way?"

"I compose. Badly. What's yours?"

"I'm a doctor," said Howson after a moment's hesitation.

"I'd never have guessed. We ought to try you on Brian, maybe—an embryo sociologist we know, who's a fanatical determinist. Trying to make out that professions and trades can be correlated with physical types. Mark you, someone like you is calculated to throw a monkey wrench in the works no matter what you do for a living—sort of a wild variable. Say, you've managed to quiet them down!" He twisted on his chair to face Jay and Charma.

Howson followed his movement. Charma was lifting her newly filled glass to him. "Your doing?" she said. "Thanks!" And gulped it thirstily. Small wonder, after all the shouting she had done.

"Rudi!" Jay said, displaying his wristwatch. "Things ought to be waking up at Clara's now. Think we could drop by?"

"Good idea," said Howson's new friend. "Say, this guy here is a doctor. We ought to tell Brian and see how his face falls, no?"

"He'd never believe you," Charma said. She drained her glass.

"And even if he did," supplemented Jay, "he has more

special exceptions than conforming cases in the scheme already."

"We should prove it to him, then," insisted Rudi. "Is he going to be at Clara's this evening?"

"When did you know that man to miss a party?" countered Jay.

"OK!" Rudi turned to Howson. "That is, if you're not doing anything. I'm sorry; I seem to have made plans for you—uh—?"

"Gerry," Howson supplied. "Well, as a matter of fact . . ."

As a matter of fact I'd love to go to this party. If I want to learn to face people, I'd like to start with people like these—iconoclastic, angry about prejudice, willing to accept me even if only because I'm out of the ordinary.

"Clara won't mind an extra guest," Rudi prompted, mistaking his hesitation. "We'll take along a couple of packs of beer, and everything will be OK."

"In that case," Howson said, rising, "I'll surely come."

On the threshold, waiting while Jay and Rudi maneuvered the big packs of beer cans through the narrow door, he suggested, "Taking a cab?"

Jay gave a hoot of laughter, elbowing back the door.

"Jay, you're an unobservant bastard," said Rudi severely. "Just because you're long-legged and bursting with vitamins you think everyone shares your passion for sore feet. Now I, since I'm observant, happen to know that Gerry here has a wad of cash big enough to *buy* us a cab for the trip. Charma, get out in the gutter and pull up your skirt!"

xxiv

*H*owson was in the grip of an excitement so violently contrasted with his earlier depression that he had to try and analyze his reactions for the sake of his own peace of mind. Otherwise he would have lost much of his pleasure in subconscious worrying.

What was it that had hit him so hard? He achieved a working explanation by the time the cab stopped.

First off, he'd missed this kind of people. Which was hardly to be wondered at. One of the first benefits of an improved standard of living, as he had already been superficially aware, is to postpone the age at which a person's opinions congeal for life. Someone forced by poverty to avoid spending on enlarging his horizons the energy and time needed simply for staying alive adopted the attitudes, ready-made, of his environment. This was why students formed the backbone of so many revolutionary movements, for instance.

Improved standards of living hadn't made much impact on *his* early life. When his mother died, fifteen years previously, the effects were still filtering down to his level.

But ten minutes with Rudi and his friends had informed him that this was something he wanted to catch up on, and he had a chance not to be missed.

When Rudi picked up Howson's bag for him and gave him a hand out of the cab, he didn't raise an objection. It wasn't a reminder of his plight, somehow. Not this time, in this company.

As he scrambled up the narrow, ill-lit staircase of the apartment house they had come to, he found himself wondering whether people who hadn't accepted the conventional attitudes toward cripples were also free of prejudice about telepathists. But he didn't feel inclined to find out immediately. That was too delicate a subject; he'd better postpone it for a while.

Detachment returned to temper his wave of heady enthusiasm, however, when he had been at the party an hour or so. The premises were small—a bed-sitting room, with minuscule kitchen adjacent and a shared toilet on the landing—and there were a *lot* of people crammed into the place. Not, apparently, including Brian, the man he was supposed to meet, but including a great many other students from the university.

For the first few minutes he was shown around as a wrench to be tossed into Brian's works. Then, though, after a rapid series of introductions, the three who had brought him became embroiled in conversation with older friends and left him to his own devices.

He was at two disadvantages then: his stature made it hard for other people to keep him in on an argument unless they were sitting and he was standing, and there was little room left to sit anywhere but on the floor; moreover, his voice was weak and hard to follow at the best of times, and here there was a tremendous amount of noise to combat—voices raised in violent disagreement, cups and glasses and bottles clattering, even before someone arrived with a concertina and began to play regardless of who cared to listen.

He was beginning to feel lost and out of place when he noticed that someone had vacated a few square inches of the edge of the sofa bed, next to the wall. He sat down promptly before he missed the opportunity; someone came by and poured him a fresh drink, and after that no one paid him any attention for some while.

He occupied himself in eavesdropping telepathically on a number of the conversations; it was impolite, but it was too interesting to be forgone. It was obvious that the new branch of the university was a very good one, and the instruction must be of high quality. Even the well-adapted telepathists among the students he had associated with in Ulan Bator hadn't displayed such keenness in the use of their intellect.

Of course, the comparison was hardly fair. All the student telepathists he had known well were outnumbered by the crowd in this one room.

Group A (he categorized them in the course of a brief survey): two girls in yellow, apparently sisters, and a man of twenty-five or so; subject under examination, religion as a necessity of human social evolution. Group B: Jay, whom he knew, a long-haired boy still in his teens, another with a slight stammer getting in the way of his arguments, and a plain girl with bangs; subject, a revue for which Jay was being persuaded to do the decor. Group C: a beautiful girl of twenty and a man in a red sweater; subject, each other. Howson felt a stir of envy and firmly diverted his attention.

Group D: four men with very loud voices standing close to the concertina player; subject, sparked off by the instrument, the influence of new musical devices on the work of contemporary composers. One of the group kept trying to talk about his own work, and the others kept forcibly steering him away from it. (Where was Rudi, anyway? Oh, yes; circling the room pouring drinks.)

Group E: two girls, one slightly drunk, and two men; subject, the drunker girl's views on modern poetry. Group F: three men, two in open shirts and one in a sweater; subject, the impossibility of living up to one's ideals in later life.

And so on. Howson was flirting dangerously with the idea of joining in one of these conversations (any of them bar Group C) by telepathic means, when he realized the suggestion probably came out of his latest drink and stopped himself with a sigh. Looking about him with his physical eyesight, he became aware that a girl had sat down next to him while he was distracted, and was now looking at him with an amused expression. She was young and rather attractive, despite wearing a blue cardigan which clashed horribly with the green of her eyes.

"Good evening," she said with mocking formality. "Meet me. I'm your hostess."

Howson sat up. "I'm sorry!" he began. "Rudi and Jay insisted on my coming—"

"Oh, you're welcome," she said, dismissing the point with a wave. "I'm the one who ought to apologize for neglecting a guest so long. I just haven't had a spare moment. Are you enjoying yourself?"

"Tremendously, thanks."

"I thought you might be, behind that mask of non-engagement. What were you doing—drinking in atmosphere?"

"Actually I was thinking what a lot of impressive and lively discussion there was here."

"Bloody, isn't it? At any party like this people dream up a dozen wonderful world-changing schemes, and they never put them into practice. Well, we should worry; been happening for centuries and it's likely to go on. Might be a good idea to note down some of the schemes and publish them—get them to someone who could make use of them. . . ." She unfocused her eyes, as though studying a future possibility. "Might have a crack at it.

But that's probably just another of those same vanishing schemes."

"Are you a writer?" Howson guessed.

"Potential. Somebody tell you?"

"No. But you have a lot of creative people here."

The girl (her name would be Clara, since she was the hostess) offered him a cigarette. He refused, but borrowed someone else's burning one to light hers with. Where the hell had he got that trick from? He'd never done it in his life before. Out of a movie, maybe, from . . . from . . .

It was with a start he recollected that he was in the same city where he had seen that movie.

"No; me," Clara was saying, "I suffer from a congenital dissatisfaction with words. I mean—hell, if you tried to explore fully just the few people here during the few hours the party lasted, you'd wind up with an unmanageable monster. How long does *Ulysses* last, for instance—eighteen hours, is it? And you still couldn't be sure you were communicating with your audience. What I'd like is a technique which would enable a pre-Columbian Amerind to understand a twentieth-century Chinese. Then—brother! I'd be a writer!"

She chuckled at the grandiosity of her own ambition, and changed the subject.

"How about you? What's your line?"

"I'm a doctor," Howson said after considering and dismissing the idea of sounding her out on the possibilities of telepathy as a solution to the problem in communication she had propounded. "Matter of fact, Rudi wanted me to come along to meet someone trying to correlate physical types with trades and professions. Brian—someone."

"Oh, yes. Rudi's forever trying to deflate him. I imagine he needed some mental acrobatics to fit you into the pattern, didn't he?"

"I don't know. I haven't been introduced to him yet."

"Well, if that isn't Rudi all over! Damn it, Brian's been here the better part of an hour. . . . Oh, maybe he'll remember and bring you together sooner or later. Do you mind? Or would you rather get it over and go?"

Howson shook his head. "I'm enjoying this," he affirmed.

Someone tapped his arm and held a bottle over his now empty glass; he covered it quickly with his palm to indicate a refusal, and then turned to put it on a handy table. For a while there was a companionable silence between them, while the party's chatter and music circled around like the winds enclosing a hurricane's eye.

xxv

*F*inally, since Clara showed no immediate desire to move on, he stirred and glanced at her.

"Who and what, exactly, is Rudi?" he asked. He was rather more interested in Rudi than in the other two he had met in the bar this evening. He had not trespassed in the younger man's mind, of course; a single telepathic sweep would have told him all he wanted to know, but he shrank from the notion as he shrank from invading anyone's mental privacy without invitation or necessity. Even on the strength of externals, however, Rudi impressed him as having a deeper and more mature personality than his friends.

"Rudi?" Clara blew smoke through her nostrils. "Rudi Allef is his full name. He's half Israeli. He came here on a UN grant. He was doing—well, *I* think he was doing—some good work. Unfortunately it wasn't the work he was supposed to do to qualify for the grant he was getting. So they discontinued it. So Jay and Charma Horne—"

"Jay and Charma Horne? Brother and sister?"

Clara stared at him. "Whatever gave you that extraordinary idea? They're married."

"*Married?*"

"Well, why shouldn't they be?"

Howson recovered himself and shrugged; he didn't do it too well, for reasons connected with the curvature of his spine. "It was just the way they were bickering with each other when I first met them. Sorry, go on."

"Ah-h-h . . . yes. So Jay and Charma, being slightly crazy anyway as you might expect in view of their having got married under the circumstances, quit in sympathy and aren't finding life any too easy. Still, you were asking about Rudi, not the Hornes. Rudi is . . . well, a problem."

"Odd you should say that," Howson remarked, puzzled "Obviously you know him better than I do, but I'd have said he seemed like a well-balanced and integrated person."

"He gives that impression, certainly." Clara looked across the room to where the object of their discussion sat on the floor near the concertina player. "Maybe one of these days, if he keeps the act up long enough, he'll convince himself that's the way he really is. And a good thing, too. Otherwise he'll suffer a serious breakdown and not be much good to himself or anybody else for a long, long time."

Momentarily unsure whether they were talking about the same person, Howson stared. "Does he show signs of cracking?" he demanded.

She seemed to draw her mind back from elsewhere, and shook herself very slightly. "Oh, if you know where to look. . . . I ought to circulate and attend to my guests, I suppose. See you later."

She had just risen to her feet when she hesitated. "I don't mean to be rude," she said. "But you seem to be a bit of a problem yourself. Are you?"

Howson looked her as hard in the eye as he could. "You claim to be good at spotting problems," he answered. "Make up your own mind."

She flushed. "I deserved that," she admitted, and turned away.

After which, Howson realized, he still didn't know much about Rudi Allef.

But at that moment Rudi himself remembered the bomb he had wanted to place under Brian's sociological theory. He climbed to his feet, dragged Brian out of the argument he was involved in, and presented Howson to him. More than ever, as he looked at Rudi's eager grin, Howson found himself tempted to take a quick peep—just one!—inside that well-shaped head.

And if he did, and proceeded inadvertently to display a knowledge of Rudi he couldn't possibly have obtained ordinarily in the course of such a short acquaintance . . . ? Howson suddenly realized what it must be like for a mulatto "passing" in a place where such things counted, and the room grew cold.

He just hadn't known this feeling before. He was an undersize cripple; all right, these people were defiantly taking so much for granted. But even here there might be those who would consider him alien. Maybe, when the time came for them to find out who he really was (and that time would inevitably come, whether he was still among them or not), they would shrug and maintain their open-mindedness. On the other hand, maybe they wouldn't.

Perhaps, in sheer self-defense, he ought to find out their opinions before committing himself? He could do it in a moment!

Then he realized he had failed to catch something that was said to him, and reflexively picked the words out of Rudi's mind. He was halfway through his answer before he realized what he had done, and the room grew even colder. He was so used to being among people from whom his talent was no secret that he had acquired many automatic habits such as that. The shock made him stumble in his reply, but he recovered quickly enough to hide his alarm.

The one glimpse inside Rudi's mind had made the idea of probing deeper still more tempting, but he told himself carefully: *He's not my patient, not a professional colleague. I may have gone too far already; no further!*

He forced himself to concentrate on the conversation. Brian, whom he didn't like at all, was shaking off his harassed mood and returning to his old comfortable dogmas. "After all," he was saying, "people like Dr. Howson here are bound to be exceptions wherever you try to fit them in. I mean, they're like trying to predict the next atom due to disintegrate in a chunk of uranium. You know one of them is going to pop, but you can't say which. Equally, you know that Dr. Howson has to fit in somewhere, but you couldn't predict where without a lot of other data. . . ."

He droned on, while Howson's mind took hold of one short phrase and worried it over and over.

"Dr. Howson has to fit in somewhere!"

It was very much later when Clara sat down near him again. The room was far less crowded; some people had gone home, and others had apparently decided to camp out on the stairs.

"Oh, that Rudi!" she said in a tone which mingled annoyance with tolerant long-suffering. "He's out in the kitchen being miserable. You'd never think it to look at him, of course. He's giving imitations of the stuffed shirts on the university staff, with props, and about half a dozen idiots are laughing at him."

"If you wouldn't think it to look at him, how would you know?" said Howson bluntly. Then a possibility occurred to him, and he caught himself. "I'm sorry. Presumably you know him very well."

"If you think he's my—well, shall we be polite and say 'intimate friend'?—you're wrong," Clara countered in a cool, slightly reproachful voice. "As a matter of fact, I hardly knew him except by sight until this thing of his grant being stopped came up a short while ago."

She paused, looking puzzled. "Come to think of it, I probably shouldn't be so . . ."

Howson shared her puzzlement. He had jumped to the exact conclusion Clara had just disabused him of; even though it didn't fit quite all the facts, it was the most obvious explanation. But if that wasn't the truth, what the—?

Several people came out of the kitchen, laughing heartily, surrounding Rudi and clapping him on the back. Howson scanned the dark, good-looking face. No, it betrayed no hint of the misery Clara claimed to detect.

While his companions took their leave, reducing the number of survivors to a mere dozen or so, Rudi helped himself from a handy bottle without seeming to care much what was in it, and went back into the kitchen. Howson assumed he had gone to rejoin somebody. He looked around the room, trying to ignore the girl and the man in the red sweater, who had progressed far beyond conversation as a means of showing their interest in each other.

"You seem, as I said before," Clara remarked as she came back to him after seeing off the departing guests, "to have—to *be*—a problem. Yes, I've made up my own mind on the point. What's worse, I've had to discard all the nice simple reasons to account for it. After all, you can't be too badly handicapped if you're a doctor. Correct?"

Her green eyes were very penetrating. Howson felt a prickle on his nape, and it had nothing to do with her reference to his deformity. With an attempt at lightness, he said, "Do you put all your guests through detailed interrogation?"

"Only the uninvited ones who intrigue me," she said, unperturbed. "Like you, for instance."

Howson suspended his intention to answer for a few seconds. A possibility had struck him which seemed on the face of it so unlikely that he was literally afraid to formulate it even to himself. He was still debating it when—

The shock almost threw him forward to the floor. The intensity of it blinded him completely; it raged inside his skull like a fire. He knew what it was, of course. Even before he had fully regained his senses, he found himself shouting, "In the kitchen! It's Rudi!"

Everyone in the room looked around in blank astonishment. And Howson realized that there hadn't been a sound.

Everyone in the room—except, it dawned on him, Clara. And Clara, white-faced, was already opening the kitchen door. She couldn't have reached it so quickly in answer to his words of warning. She *couldn't* have. And that meant—

She screamed.

Cursing his unresponsive body, Howson struggled to his feet. Already half a dozen astonished people were crowding with a babble of horrified cries through the kitchen door. Their voices were incoherent, and their minds were clouded with shock. It didn't matter. Howson knew perfectly well what had happened.

The voice of Brian, the would-be sociologist, rose

authoritatively above the din. "Don't touch him! Get the little guy in here—he's a doctor. And someone phone for an ambulance. Clara, is there a phone?"

'Down the basement," the girl answered in a shaky but controlled voice.

Meantime, Howson was dragging himself through five seconds of times slowed to the duration of an hour. *I'm a doctor,* he was thinking. *I know about lesions of the cerebellum. I know about maladjustment and psychosis from the inside. But what the hell good is that to a guy leaking his life away on a hard kitchen floor?*

They stood aside to let him pass, and he looked down with physical sight for the first time at something already too familiar to him. Rudi had literally and precisely committed hara-kiri (why? A tantalizing hint of explanation hovered just beyond Howson's mental reach) with a common carving knife from a nearby drawer.

Now that he was unconscious, the blinding pain signal from his mind was easier to shut out. But the pain of his own helplessness remained. These people—these people! —were looking to him for advice and guidance. . . .

He found his voice. "Anyone gone for an ambulance?"

A chorus assured him some had.

"Good. Then get out of here and shut the door. Keep as quiet as you can. Better yet, get the hell out of the apartment—no, the police may want to—oh, *blast* the police! Go home!"

Clara was moving to join the others, but he frowned and said nothing, and she heard him. Shyly she closed the door and came back to his side.

"Know anything about this sort of thing?" he said grimly.

"N-no. But I'll do anything you say. *Is* there anything we can do?"

"He'll be dead in about five minutes unless we do something." Howson laughed without humor. "And the joke is that I'm not a medical doctor. I've never so much as dressed a cut finger in my life—barring my own."

*A*t the end of an eternal silence lasting the space of three heartbeats, she absorbed the words and was able to react. To herself she said, coloring the concepts with gray despair: *Oh, God—poor, stupid Rudi!* And aloud, more fiercely, she said, "Then why did you say you were a doctor if you aren't one?"

"But I am, of a kind. And things aren't quite as bad as you're imagining. Do you know you're a receptive telepathist?"

"A *what?*" Coming on top of the shock of seeing Rudi weltering in his pool of blood and undigested liquor, the information was at first meaningless. Howson sensed a shield of incomprehension and subconscious denial, and hammered at it.

"I'm telling you, you can read people's minds. And my doctorate happens to be in curative telepathy. Got that? Good! Now, there's one person in this room who knows—perhaps—what Rudi Allef needs to heal him. And that's Rudi Allef."

She tried to interrupt, but he rushed on, abandoning the use of slow words. Instead, he slammed whole blocks of associated concepts into her mind directly.

Deep in Rudi's brain, as in all ordinary people's, there's what we call body image—a master plan the body uses for its major repairs. I'm going after it. You'll have to take instructions from me and carry them out because my hands are too clumsy for delicate work. Don't try to think for yourself—let go!

LET.

GO!

And with that, he simultaneously reached deep into Rudi's failing mind and took over control of Clara's hands.

160

She struggled, but gamely tried to overcome her instinctive resistance, and within a minute he was able to make her lift back Rudi's shoulders so they could see the gashed opening in his belly.

The sight shocked her so much Howson momentarily lost control; he spared a valuable few seconds to reassure her, and then continued his exploration of Rudi's body image.

So many of his nerves were reporting damage and pain that he could not at first distinguish between them. He decreased his sensitivity, but that only resulted in a vague blur.

He sat down on a chair and steeled himself. Then he began again.

This time it was as if the nerves were reporting their agony directly to himself, from his own body lying torn and ruined. But none of that must be relayed to Clara, for it would render her incapable of assisting him. He had to absorb and master the pain within himself. . . .

All right, now. What first? Stop the leakage of blood before the activity of the brain wasted completely away. Something . . . Clips? Hair clips? Didn't women usually have such things?

Clara had some in a bowl only a foot from her shoulder. She seized them and furiously began to clip the open ends of the major blood vessels. The weakening of the brain diminished, remained steady at an irreducible trickle.

All right. Put back the displaced intestines, so.

Covered with blood, Clara's hands seized the gray-blue living guts and settled them tenderly in place; pushed at torn mesenteries and got them back roughly where they belonged. With each action came a reduction of the pain and damage reports battering at Howson. By the time she had completed the replacement of the vital organs he was able to open his eyes. He had not realized they were shut.

"An ordinary needle and thread," he said huskily, and she got them; she left bloody hand prints on the table, on the door handle, everywhere. "Stitch the stomach wall together," he directed, and she did, clumsily by surgical standards, but well enough. "Now the skin itself; now wash your hands, wash the skin, get a clean piece of cloth to dress it—"

Rudi's mind blazed up as he returned to consciousness for an instant, unexpectedly; Howson gritted his teeth and slapped the ego back into oblivion. Rough-and-ready treatment, but then, so much damage had already been done to Rudi's personality, a little more would make no difference.

What counted was that the tiny flicker of life smoldered on. It would last until a blood transfusion; then they could repair the damage properly. Meantime, Howson had achieved all he could ask: survival.

It had taken exactly five minutes.

Now there would be the ambulance, and police, with questions. He couldn't remember if attempted suicide was still a crime here; in some places, he had a vague idea the antique Christian attitude endured. . . .

Clara came back from putting away the needle and thread, and stood gazing down at her handiwork. "Why did he have to try and kill himself?" she said half angrily, and Howson shook his head. He felt as tired as if he had walked a thousand miles, but he must not let weariness claim him.

"He didn't try to kill himself," he said. "It was an accident. It was stupid, but not suicidal. Part of a joke that went too far."

She sensed what lay behind that, in his mind, and nodded without his needing to explain further, but he had to explain when the ambulance arrived, and again when the police came, and after it all he was so exhausted he sat down in the nearest chair and went to sleep.

When he awoke, he was for a long time puzzled as to where he could be. He lay on his back between sheets, a pillow comfortably under his head. But the bed didn't have that slight ingenious bias which had been built into his own bed at Ulan Bator and which favored his back so subtly. More, the light played on the too-high ceiling in the wrong manner—

He came fully awake and turned on his side, and saw that Clara, wrapped in a plaid blanket, was dozing in the room's one armchair.

She sensed his awakening and blinked her eyes open. She didn't say anything for a few moments. Then she smiled.

"Feeling all right?" she asked banally. "You were so fast asleep you didn't even notice when I put you to bed."

"You what?"

"Did you expect me to put you on the floor?" She got to her feet, unwrapping the blanket, and stretched. She was wearing the same clothes she had had on during the party.

"I'd have been all right in the chair where I was!"

"Oh, shut up!" she said almost angrily. "You deserved the bed more than I did, by Christ. I don't want to argue about it, anyway. Feel capable of breakfast?"

Howson sat up. He found she had taken off his shoes and jacket and left him otherwise fully dressed, so he pushed aside the bedclothes and got his feet to the floor. "Well, you know—you know, I think I do."

She brought cereal and coffee and opened a can of fruit juice, and they sat eating off their knees on the edge of the unmade bed.

"What I want to know," she said after a while, "is how you managed to fob everyone off with that phony story about an accident."

Howson grunted. "If there's one thing a projective telepathist can do convincingly, it's tell a lie. I could make the average man believe the sun was out at midnight with *no* difficulty. I ought really to have fixed the same idea in the skulls of the other people who were here, for the sake of consistency, instead of ordering them off the premises. But I was so worried in case their presence distracted me . . . Oh, what the hell? None of them actually saw him do it."

He put aside the bowl from which he had been eating. "I should have asked you before. How do you feel about being a telepathist yourself?"

The green eyes held a hint of uncertainty. "Then you meant what you said? I tried to—to receive something from you last night, after the police had gone, and nothing happened, so I guessed you'd just spun me a yarn to boost my confidence. Or something," she finished lamely.

"You were probably too exhausted. I did mean what I

said, of course. Tell me something: how did you know
what Rudi had done?"

"Why, he—screamed!"

"He didn't utter a sound. He might have been a genuine Samurai. If he had screamed, everyone in the room
would have heard it. Only you and I knew what had happened beyond the closed door of the kitchen, and that
means you're a receptive telepathist. I'd already begun
to suspect that you might be; I'm surprised you hadn't
wondered about it yourself."

She finished eating and lighted a cigarette. "Oh, this
is all so . . . disturbing! I mean, I'd always thought of
telepathists as people—you know—*apart*."

"They are," confirmed Howson with quiet grimness.

"And I didn't even know there were—what do you call
them?—receptive ones."

"They do seem to be rather rare, as a matter of fact.
I suspect there are probably a lot more than we know
about. I mean, you can spot a projective telepathist easily,
if he's reasonably powerful and totally untrained; he
stands out like a fire alarm. Me"—he chuckled—"they
overheard from a satellite orbiting at six thousand miles!
but how do you spot a receptive unless something happens positively to identify him, or her?"

He leaned back against the wall. "However, you may
take all that as read, in your case. You're about the right
age for the talent to show itself, you know; mine came
on when I was twenty, and that's typical. So what are
you going to do?"

"I've no idea." She looked rather frightened. "I have-
n't even worked out how I'm going to tell my family."

"That's one problem I never had to face," Howson admitted. "Do they have prejudices, then?"

"I don't know. I mean, the subject sort of never
came up." A thought creased her brow. "Look, what the
hell do receptive telepathists *do,* anyway? Aren't they
pretty limited in their choice of work?"

"By comparison with projectives, I suppose they are,"
Howson agreed in a judicious tone. "But a telepathist is
a very special person, and the demand for their services
isn't by any means exhausted. I can tell you a few of the

standard occupations. Most of the receptives I know are psychiatric diagnosticians and therapy watchdogs—"

"'Are what?'"

He explained. "Then there's Olaf Marks, who's a genius-spotter. He loves kids, so they gave him the business of discovering outstandingly brilliant children in the preverbal stage. Then there's Makerakera, whom you may well have heard of; he's recognized by the UN as an authority on aggression, and spends his time going from one potential crisis to another identifying grievances and having them put right. Oh, don't worry about being limited in your choice of a career; we're near enough unique to be able to pick and choose."

She gave a little nervous laugh. "It's funny to hear you say 'we' and know you're including me in it! Still, what you said is quite reassuring."

"I'm not saying it to reassure you. I'm just telling you. Apart from anything else, you wouldn't be happy doing anything which didn't exploit your talent once it's fully developed. I don't want to make out that being a telepathist doesn't pose its own problems, Lord knows. . . ." Howson sighed. "You were right about me last night, as you must have guessed."

"More . . . more telepathy?"

"What do *you* think?"

She got up and began to clear away the breakfast things without answering. After an interval of silence she said, "How about Rudi, Gerry? Did you have a chance to find out what made him do it?"

"No. One has to learn not to intrude on another mind's privacy. One *has* to, or life wouldn't be worth living. And while we were patching him up, of course, I couldn't spare the time. You've had a much better chance to find out why he did it."

She made a helpless gesture. "All I could tell was that he was . . . well, living a lie, as they say. Doing it well, but . . ." She gestured to complete the statement. "Gerry, what are you doing here, anyway? You're from Ulan Bator, aren't you?"

"Yes—now. But I was born here."

"Are you looking up old acquaintances?"

"I looked up a couple. That was a failure. No, I'm

after new rather than old acquaintances. It's partly a vacation, partly a voyage of self-discovery. . . . You'll find out what I mean some day."

She accepted the hint. "So, what should I do now, to get back to my own worries?" She smiled faintly.

"Officially, you should drop by at the local World Health headquarters and take the aptitude tests. Then they'd fly you to Ulan Bator or Canberra or perhaps Hong Kong for proper training. But I'd say, give yourself time to get used to the prospect before you report in."

"You seem awfully sure I will report in, yet if I asked you not to tell anyone about me, I think you'd agree."

"Of course. Only after a while you'll get dissatisfied with your own awkwardness. You'll get frustrated with things you don't know how to handle. And one day you'll say, 'Ah, the hell with it,' and go and ask how to use your gift to the full. It wasn't telepathists who worked out the techniques, you know; it was ordinary psychologists who could no more project an impression than ride a bicycle to the moon. And now I want you to do something for me. Go down to the phone and call the hospital where they took Rudi—it's the Main General. He'll probably still be under sedation. Ask if we can— I'm sorry. Are you busy this morning?"

She shook her head.

"Then ask if we, if you want to come, can see him. Tell them I'm Gerald Howson, Psi.D., Ulan Bator. They'll fall all over themselves to let me come."

"Then why bother to call up first?"

Howson looked at her steadily. "I want them to have a chance to learn that I'm a runt with a bum leg instead of a husky superman," he said calmly. "It hurts less that way."

Clara bit her lip. "That was tactless of me," she said.

"Yes," said Howson, and got up. "I'll go and wash up while you're making that call."

R udi Allef lay in his hospital bed with a cradle to keep the bedding off his injured abdomen. He was not unconscious, but he was chiefly aware of pain. The sedatives he had been given had reduced it to a level like that of a raging headache, and enabled him for short periods to sidestep it within his mind and think coherently; however, most of the time the effort simply did not seem worthwhile.

When Howson came to him, he lay unmoving with his eyes tightly shut.

The atmosphere and apppearance of this place was very much like what he was used to at Ulan Bator, Howson found. What kept reminding him that he was actually a stranger was the ostentatious deference with which he, as a Psi.D., Ulan Bator, was treated. About half the staff had attempted to accompany him to Rudi's ward, but he had shown temper for the first time in a long while and refused to permit anyone to come with him except the surgeon who had operated on Rudi and the senior ward nurse. And Clara, naturally.

He could tell she was uncomfortable. Now that she was aware of her gift, she was more able to receive the impressions it brought her, and she had not yet learned when in a hospital to concentrate on the undercurrent of healing beneath the ever-present sensations of pain. In memory of his own beginnings, he loaned her self-confidence with his mind.

They came into the ward. Screens were drawn around the bed where Rudi lay with a rubber pipe taped to his arm; the last of several transfusions to make up his loss of blood was just ending.

The nurse parted the screens, let the visitors through,

and drew them close again. There was a chair ready for Howson by the bed; awkwardly, because it was full-sized, he scrambled on to it and peered into Rudi's mind.

Meantime he spoke in words to the surgeon, saying, "What sort of state was he in when you operated?"

"Bad," said the surgeon, a straight-bodied woman of forty. "He'd have been dead if it hadn't been for the first aid you gave him. It was just as well you were there, Dr. Howson—though I didn't know curative telepathists ever had a full-scale medical course."

"I never did," Howson answered. And repeated, "I'd never more than bandaged a cut finger before."

He could feel resentment hardening in her as the words sank in; it meant, "Not only is this little cripple possessed of superior powers; he can do my job for me without training, without trouble, and boast about his success. . . ."

"That's hardly a fair thought," Howson said mildly. "I'm sorry, but it's not, you know!"

Clara, who had been listening with puzzlement, interrupted unexpectedly. "You should have seen what it cost him! The pain he must have—"

Clara! The single warning thought cut off her hasty words.

"All right," he said aloud. "May I have silence, please?"

Rudi . . .

The figure on the bed stirred very slightly. That was the only visible clue to his reaction. But inside his head he was answering.

What do you want, you interfering bastard?

I saved your life, Rudi.

For what? For pain like this? You condemned me to it when you interfered and stopped me from doing what I meant to do.

Howson took a deep breath. He had said earlier to Clara that a projective telepathist could tell a lie convincingly; now he summoned up all his reserves to prove the corollary—that he could convincingly tell the truth.

I know, Rudi. I can feel that pain as sharply as you, remember? I'm fully aware of what I've done to you. Now I must give you something to compensate: happi-

ness, or satisfaction, whatever you want that I can let you have. Otherwise how would my conscience treat me?

The whole mind was involved in this. Behind the verbalized projection, smoothly, automatically, Howson fed in a reflection of Rudi's suffering, filtered through his own mind, impressed with his own personality.

A feeble flicker of disbelief: *But you're nothing to me. We're strangers, and today we might have been a thousand miles apart.*

Nobody is nothing to one of us. And behind that, because it was too complex to put into words, Howson made himself feel consciously feel what was usually so much a part of himself that he never gave it a thought—the shared quality of a telepathist's existence, the need and hunger and yearning which were all the ordinary individual's needs and hungers and yearnings a millionfold multiplied, as if in a hall of mirrors by reflection redoubling and redoubling themselves away toward infinity.

This was why a telepathist became a peacemaker, or a psychiatrist, or a curative telepathist, or a disputes arbitrator—helping people to be happier or better off or more fulfilled. It was also why he had been eager to tell splendid glamorous telepathic stories to the deaf-and-dumb girl he now knew as Mary Williams, and why he had been so bitterly disappointed to learn that the pleasure had turned into a Greek gift.

It was also why (though ordinary people were always suspicious of the assertion unless they had been shown its truth by someone like Howson) there had never been a telepathist who was antisocial, who became a master criminal or general of an army. No telepathist could stand in the place of Chaka Zulu and order his hordes to ravage a season's journey in the direction in which he cast his spear; no telepathist could consign fellow beings to a gas chamber, or annihilate them in atomic war. They were too human to have shed all desire for power, but to enjoy it they had to take the road into the isolation of madness; in the real world they suffered their victims' pain, and had no pleasure from cruelty.

It was also the naked truth.

Rudi's eyes flickered open, and he looked at the

vacuous face masking the keen mind. Last night, when
they first met, he had ignored the conventional reaction
to Howson's small stature, deformity, unprepossessing appearance—but because on principle he ignored the con-
ventions which demanded the reactions. He was half
Israeli; perhaps his people had a legacy of conventional
prejudices enough to last them for eternity—all directed
against them. So, by analogy, he would have leaned
over backward to avoid offending a Negro. So would
millions of people; only most of them, if they failed to
learn the logic of prejudice, learned the logic of self-
interest and therefore conformed. Rudi would not.

He yielded now to the pressure of pain; it was easy to
slip back into the fog of despair. For Howson, it was
very hard to follow him, but it had to be done—and he
had done it often in the past.

Why did you do it, Rudi?

A complex picture of dissatisfaction with the work he
had set himself to do; with the reception it had had; with
the inability of other people to understand what he was
doing. Add to that: money troubles, because of the
stopping of his grant; emotional problems on a personal
level—he needed the affection and acceptance of a woman,
any woman who could understand his needs; he was
good-looking and pleasant, but that was not enough to
secure the right partner. He had tried many, and the last
had been cruel. And the mask he had put up to protect
himself against the scrutiny of the world had proved his
undoing; people who could not penetrate it, and therefore
had no idea of the turmoil of sorrow boiling in his
brain, had been tactless, unkind, reopening old sores
without realizing.

So he had picked up a knife, and thought how much
he would like oblivion.

But Howson could see behind the mask, and therefore would not be tactless and unkind; he understood
Rudi's needs, and could help and advise him. He dismissed the superficialities, such as money trouble, with
an impatient mental gesture, and went straight ahead to
the factor which all through Rudi's bitter survey of his
reasons for suicide had taken the foremost place: his work.

What work is this?

Chaos, mingled with striving. Behind it all, very deep, was a need to create and bring forth. Howson found it amazingly feminine, much reminiscent of certain urges he had known in the deep unconscious of frustrated single women. From this sprang several consequences; he saw them presented all at once, but had to verbalize them in succession.

Though feminine, this impulse was also general-human. It had by-products which he merely noted and filed for reference—such as the reason why Rudi's creativity gave him agony (his deep unconscious saw it as parturition, and that brings pain), and the reason why he chose to attempt suicide by hara-kiri (it represented a Caesarian delivery on the cross-reference identity level of his mind).

But Rudi's deep unconscious could only inform the probing inquisitorial mind why he needed to create; it did not explain the nature of the creative activity, and the way in which the conscious was tackling it. Howson drew back, dizzying for a moment as he discovered his own body to be cramped and stiff. Small wonder; this chair was a poor substitute for the special bed from which he usually worked. Still, no matter.

"There's too much pain," he told the surgeon shortly. "Would it be safe for him to get a local in the stomach wall?"

Then he focused his physical vision, and found that the nurse had already lifted up the bedclothes and was preparing to give an injection. He looked blankly at her. Then, struck by a sudden realization, he turned to Clara, who stood white-faced with her hands on the bar at the foot of the bed.

She read the question before he could utter it, and nodded. "You told me about therapy watchdogs. So I—uh—already asked for him to be given the anesthetic."

Howson felt a deep wave of appreciation and gratitude; he did not check it, but projected it as it stood, and Clara flushed with embarrassment.

How do you feel?

Oh, Gerry—it's magnificent, but it's somehow absolutely terrifying, too!

Howson hesitated. Then, as if confessing a serious error of judgment, he said in words, "You know, I might have been wrong this morning. Maybe you won't have to ask anyone to teach you how to use your gift properly."

The nurse and the surgeon exchanged puzzled glances at this unforeshadowed remark.

"But"—Clara seemed just as astonished—"but *you're* teaching me! You're teaching me all the time!"

xxviii

*H*owson was still pondering that when the nurse gently touched Rudi's bandaged abdomen. He did not wince. "The local's taken effect, Dr. Howson," she said quietly.

"Fine." With an effort Howson returned to the work in hand.

Rudi!

Yes? A pure conscious note of interrogation, blended with assent and willingness to cooperate now he had sensed the telepathist's power.

And Howson settled down to find clarity and order in something that was not clear to Rudi himself.

Springing from this fundamental creative urge were the reasons why it could not find an outlet in writing, painting, sculpture, or anything else where the creator was divorced from his audience. Rudi could never be satisfied to devise something and leave other people, elsewhere, to appreciate it. Appreciation fed and renewed his desire to create, as an actor feeds on a "good audience" and rises to new interpretative heights.

And yet acting, again, would be inadequate for Rudi because it *was* interpretative. So was ballet; so was almost every other form of art in which there was the direct audience contact Rudi craved—although he had been a first class debater, conjuring up splendid impromptu ora-

tions. (Howson had to sift through a dozen such quali-
fications and explanations before he arrived at a clear
picture of what Rudi was actually trying to do.)

Essentially, though, it was music which attracted him
most. And—

And Howson found himself on the top of a dizzying
slide, lost his grip, and went headlong, skidding and slipping into a vast uncharted jungle of interlocked sensory
experiences.

Rudi Allef's mind was almost as far from the ordinary
as was Howson's own, but in a different direction. Somehow, Rudi's sense data cross-referred interchangeably.
Howson had experience of minds with limited audio-
vision—those of people to whom musical sounds called
up associated colors or pictures—but compared to what
went on in Rudi's mind that was puerile.

(Once, long before, he had seen a tattered print of
Disney's *Fantasia;* he had enjoyed it. and had wished
there had been more attempts to combine sound and vision in a similar way. Now he was finding out what the
combination could be like on the highest level.)

Like a swimmer struggling in a torrential river, Howson
sought wildly for solidity in this roaring stream of memory.
Images presented themselves: a voice/velvet/a kitten's
claws scratching/purple/ripe fruit—a ship's siren/fog/
steel/yellowish-gray/cold/insecurity/sense of loss and
emptiness—a common chord of C major struck on a
piano/childhood/wood/black and white overlaid with
bright gold/hate/something burning/tightness about the
forehead/shame/stiffness in the wrists/liquidity/round-
ness . . .

There was virtually no end to that one. Howson drew
back a little and tried again.

He was walking through a forest of ferns a hundred
feet high with gigantic animals browsing off their bark;
he was rather tired, as if he had come a long way, and the
sun was extremely hot. But he came to a blue river and
became an ice floe bobbing on a gentle current, melting
slowly into the water around. He-the water plunged over
a precipice; the pain of striking rock after rock in the long
descent was somehow satisfying and fulfilling because he

was standing back watching the white spray as he flowed down and there was a solidity being worn away as the water eroded the underlying rocks and the spray diffused out with vastness and blackness and far down below a sensation of warmth and redness not seen but imagined (infraredness?) as though he was on an airless world with a red sun, a giant red sun, crawling over the horizon to turn into something scuttering and four-legged on an endless black plain which was only a few feet across and around which giants, unheeding, went about their business with bass footsteps and bass voices . . .

Only all the time he was listening to an orchestra.

Howson felt very tired. Someone was slapping his cheeks gently with a towel dipped in ice water. He opened his eyes and found he was still on the chair by Rudi's bed.

"Are you all right?" said Clara anxiously, peering over the shoulder of the nurse who was wielding the wet towel. "You—you were frightened . . . ?"

"How long was I away?" demanded Howson in a hoarse voice.

"It's been nearly three hours," said the surgeon, glancing at her watch.

"Less than I thought; still, you were right to pull me back." Howson got gingerly to his feet and took a step to ease the pins-and-needles in his legs. He glanced at Clara.

What did you make of it?

I don't quite know. . . . There was a lot of fear.

Your own. Howson frowned. Something wouldn't come clear to consciousness—something he had half sensed in the chaos of Rudi's mental imagery. Still, it was no good trying to rush things. He spoke aloud to the surgeon.

"Thank you for letting me study him. I hope I haven't put a strain on him. Would you check how well he stood it, and say how soon you think he'll be able to face full-scale therapy?"

"Are you proposing to treat him here?" said the surgeon. She was torn between being flattered that a curative telepathist of such renown should want to work here, and annoyance at the intrusion of an outsider. Flattery won; Howson made gently sure of that.

She checked Rudi thoroughly and swiftly. "Pulse strong;

blood pressure not too bad; respiration fair . . ." She rolled back an eyelid and flashed a light into the pupil. "Yes, Dr. Howson, he seems to have stood up to it well. He should be strong enough for you in . . . well, at a fair guess, a week to ten days."

Howson repressed his disappointment. He wanted to get to grips with Rudi's fascinating mind as soon as possible. How would he contain himself for a full week after the tantalizing glimpse of riches in that mental store?

Well, that would have to take care of itself.

He and Clara found a restaurant near the hospital and sat long over a meal and several cups of coffee, while he sorted out his memories of Rudi's mind and put them up clearly and in order for her to inspect. But the prolonged strain began to mist her perception, so they reverted to words at last.

"Poor Rudi," Clara said, absently stirring emptiness in her coffee cup. "No wonder he was so frustrated. . . . How can he ever hope to communicate with an audience?"

"Oh, I know he recognizes that no one else shares precisely his association of one sensation with another. In one sense, a telepathist is the only ideal audience for him. But consciously he would be satisfied if he could create a passable objective facsimile of his mental images, to which his audience could add their own associations. What he can't reconcile himself to is the fact that, since practically no one else can perform feats of mental cross-connection on such a grand scale, no one has ever seen exactly what he was driving at."

"Until you?" suggested Clara.

"Until me. Put it in concrete terms. You've mentioned his run-in with the university authorities. I take it he was doing experimental composition of some kind, though not the kind of thing the authorities expected. Right?"

Clara nodded. "Some of it was really weird! But they might have put up with that. The main trouble came when he enlisted Jay Horne's support. He started, as they said, interfering with Jay's own work, which is far more accessible, and they warned him not to take up so much of Jay's time. That was what sparked the row and led to the cancellation of his grant. At least, so Charma told me; I've known her longer than Jay."

"I see. So anyway, it goes like this: Rudi produces an experimental work, whose logic is that of his own associations and not that of the orchestral sounds. He'd be satisfied with even minimal comprehension on the part of the listener; instead, his audience listens only for the sake of the sounds themselves, thus missing the whole point of the work. His hopes dwindle. He gets more and more helpless even when he deliberately restricts the range of associations on which he bases his music, and as he approaches nearer to the conventional, he more and more feels that he's abandoning what he wants—rather, needs—to achieve.

"If he enlists Jay's help, it's because he's cut himself down to the absolute bearable minimum. Discarding all other sensory cross references such as those he himself experiences, he thinks he might as well convey plain images of color and movement rather than nothing at all. Right? I haven't a very clear impression of Jay's work, except for the description Rudi gave me, but he made me feel he didn't regard it too highly."

"He does, though. He doesn't regard Jay himself too highly, which isn't the same thing."

"Hmmm!" Howson rubbed his chin. "But the difficulty one always runs up against in every attempt to integrate music and visual impressions is that the machinery is expensive, complicated and generally inadequate. What one needs is an instrument as simple and versatile as a piano, which combines the resources of a color-organ with those of an unlimited film library."

Clara stared at him. "Do you know, those are almost exactly the same words that Charma once used to me when things were going badly between Rudi and Jay?"

"Not surprising. Probably they were the words Rudi himself used." Howson stared into space. "Clara, let's go and call on the Hornes. There are things I ought to know before I try any therapy for Rudi."

"You said," Clara reminded him timidly, "you were on a vacation?"

"A man at Ulan Bator hospital asked me why I didn't use my talents for my own satisfaction," said Howson with a hint of bitterness. "So that's what I propose to do. I can't deny that I look forward to seeing Rudi Allef thank me for all I've done for him. Only first I've got to find something I *can* do for him. Let's go."

xxix

$\mathcal{J}$ ay and Charma lived in a two-room apartment on the top of an old house not far from Grand Avenue. The air was full of dust from the demolition work in progress nearby. When the visitors arrived, Charma was attempting to cope with the additional housework this caused under a barrage of furious complaints from Jay about the disturbance to his precious equipment. Howson and Clara exchanged glances; they could sense the raised tempers from outside the door.

However, they knocked and were let in, and when Charma had cleared off a couple of chairs and conjured a pot of coffee out of the wrecked-looking kitchenette, Howson realized that he could detect a harmony of attitude between the couple which underlay and supported their superficial eternal disagreement. It rather took him aback, but evidently it was a workable arrangement.

He repressed the desire to probe further and stated the purpose of their call. It wasn't until he had almost finished that he realized neither Jay nor Charma knew who he really was. He explained, wondering what their reaction would be.

"Good *grief!*" said Jay, his mild blue eyes growing round with astonishment. "Talk about angels unawares! When I think where poor old Rudi would be now, if it hadn't been for you! Thanks, Dr. Howson. I think he was worth saving. He's going places—even if he does get on my nerves."

"Call me Gerry," said Howson, relieved beyond measure at the ready acceptance Jay revealed. "Anyway, I came hoping to see something of what you and Rudi have been doing together."

"That's no trouble. Charma, honey, suppose you clear the piano and get out that thing we were looking at yesterday. I'll turn on the gadgets."

At one side of the small, crowded room there stood a battered upright piano; Howson hadn't noticed it for the tangle of electrical and other equipment hanging down over it. When Charma cleared it off, he saw that it wasn't quite an ordinary piano: it had two additional keyboards, one governing an organ-simulator and the other controlling a battery of strips of tape, each with a separate playing head.

"That's for special effects," explained Jay as he went from point to point in the room, turning switches. "Rudi is hell for getting everything just so. Now, here's my own particular pet." And he took the wooden lid off a large glass box like an aquarium, at the bottom of which a pool of luminescent fluid gleamed faintly. A row of colored lights shone down each side of the tank.

"Lights down," said Jay, taking his place at a haywire panel of electrical controls. There was darkness as Charma hauled the curtains across the window; by the eerie green glow of the luminous liquid, Howson saw her sit down at the piano.

"Watch the tank," Jay said briefly. "OK, honey—one, two, three."

A succession of irregular intervals down the keyboard, ending in a swelling peal of bells from one of the special keys, and shapes began to form in the glass tank: multi-colored, responding vaguely and randomly to the music. Within a few seconds they were growing definite, and hard square forms followed hard square chords.

Watching intently, Howson thought he detected a shallow, distorted resemblance to certain things he had seen in Rudi's mind, but how elementary this makeshift was compared to the vivid, far-reaching volumes of association he had perceived there!

The music stopped. "That's as far as we got with that one," said Jay coolly. "Open the curtains, there's a dear."

And as Charma let in the light, he looked at Howson. He raised an inquiring eyebrow.

"It's clever," said Howson. "But it's much too limited for really ambitious treatment."

Jay looked delighted. "Precisely what I've been saying. I've gone along with almost everything Rudi has asked me to do, because he's a genuine creative artist and I'm a tinker. But he's taken up a hell of a lot of my time, and we don't seem to have been very happy collaborators. If you'll come into the other room, I'll show you what I'm doing myself."

In the other room there were dozens of the glass tanks ranged on shelves, some of them dusty, all dark and unprepossessing. Jay went to an electric outlet and plugged in a wandering cord.

"My 'wet fireworks,' as my beloved wife will insist on calling them," he murmured. "Watch—this is my latest."

He connected the cord to a socket beneath one of the larger tanks. A faint light came on; after a pause, it brightened, and a stream of opalescent bubbles began to work their way through the tank in a switchback formation. Shafts of green, yellow and blue shifted through the tank in an irregular series of graceful loops; then a square form in bright red loomed up from a point till it almost filled the side of the tank nearest to the watchers. It vanished, and the graceful swerving curves continued.

"It never repeats itself," said Jay thoughtfully. "It's like a kaleidoscope—in fact, I guess that's what it most resembles."

"It's much more successful than what you've been doing with Rudi," said Howson. "But its scope isn't so great."

Jay connected another of the tanks; this one was darker—dark red, midnight blue and purple shot with heavy gold and rare flashes of white. His eyes fixed on it, he nodded. "And yet this is what I'm trying to do," he said. "I'm after something quite simple: I just want to convey movement and color in a . . . well, in a beautiful combination. Or an ugly one, for that matter. Like this!" He snapped a switch, and a third tank lighted up— hesitantly moving, abrupt in its changes of color, the drab pattern dissolving frequently into muddy brown and a sickly olive-gray.

"But you see," he continued, "*I* know what I'm after. Sometimes I've had the impression Rudi doesn't. I mean, I'd follow his instructions to the letter, spending hours over a single effect, and then have him go through the roof because it wasn't what he wanted after all."

"I'm not surprised," Howson said musingly. "Rudi's sensory impressions are so interlocked that I doubt if he can visualize anything straightforwardly. He hears a chord struck on your piano, and he immediately links it up with—oh, let's say the taste and texture of a slice of bread, the color of a stormy sky, and the smell of stagnant water, together with a bodily sensation of anxiety and pins-and-needles in the left arm. All these interlock with still other ideas. Result—chaos! He probably can't single out the different items; he can't separate the color of the sky from the color of the greenish weed on the water or the bread color of the bread. He mingles them all together. But no one else could possibly take them in simultaneously and achieve the same associations that he gets."

"Except you," said Clara.

"Yes," Howson agreed, his eyes on her. "Except me. Or another telepathist . . . Jay, what are the resources of that gadget in the room where we were just now?"

"Aside from the obvious limits imposed by the speed of response—and its small size, of course—pretty well inexhaustible. We've worked on it, on and off, for almost a year. At the moment it's programmed for a particular item, but it can be controlled manually, too."

"I see. Right. Let me think for a while, will you?" Howson leaned his elbow on a vacant shelf and closed his eyes, knowing that Jay and Charma would assume he was thinking for his own attention only. In fact . . .

Clara! Tell me something, will you? Why was it that you took such an interest in Rudi if you scarcely knew him?

Why . . . A sense of embarrassment and uncertainty. *I guess I felt sorry for him. . . ?*

Be honest with me. It's bigger than that, isn't it? You find him attractive, don't you?

Y-yes . . .

In fact, you'd like to know him a lot better. And the idea that you might wind up by falling in love with him has crossed your mind, hasn't it?

You're a peeping tom! But there was no real annoyance in the sentiment; clearly, she found the idea very acceptable.

Howson grinned like a Cheshire cat. He opened his eyes and glanced at Jay.

"Can you spare the time to do a little more work on that machine of yours?" he inquired, and on noting a momentary hesitation, hurried on. "Look, it's going to get you out of your impasse with Rudi. I agree with you—he's going places. Given the right opportunity, he could create what amounts to a new channel of artistic expression. It won't happen overnight; it'll take time and enough public interest to make resources available so that he can integrate sight, sound, smell, maybe even more complex imagery. What he needs right now, though, is chiefly hope. And I believe I know how we can give him that."

Rudi!

Howson felt the mind shrink a little and then remember. The healing was progressing well; Howson felt a stir of envy at the healthy normality of Rudi's bodily functions. He could never have sustained an injury one-tenth as bad as the one the younger man was recovering from.

They had moved Rudi into a private soundproof room, and now they were all here: Jay, Charma and Clara, with a nurse standing by. Howson renewed his approach gently.

Rudi, think of your music.

As though floodgates had opened, a wave of imagined sound poured into Rudi's aching consciousness. Howson fought to channel and control it. When he had gained the minimal mastery he needed, he signaled to Clara.

The tank—which had taken four men to bring it into the room—lighted up. Clara, a strained look on her face, flashed the controls, and Howson suggested that Rudi open his eyes. He did so; he saw. . . .

Jay and Charma, of course, could not hear the music

that pulsed and raged in Rudi's mind. But Howson could, and so could Clara, and that was what mattered.

They had spent the week experimenting, improving and training; now the tank's speed of response was phenomenal, and Jay had improvised new, simpler controls to make the device as versatile and essentially as straightforward as a theremin. And Clara . . .

Howson had wondered sometimes in the course of the time they had spent together whether it was just that she was a ready subject, or that he was himself a remarkable instructor in telepathy, for she was reading Rudi's fantastic mental projections, sifting them and extracting their essentials, *and* converting them to visual images, as fast as Rudi himself could think them.

Awed amazement was plain on Rudi's face as he watched the tank. Jay and Charma, who could not hear the music to which Clara was responding, were almost as startled. And Howson felt purely overjoyed.

Mountains grew in the tank, distorted as if looked at from below, purple-blue and overpowering; mists gathered at their peaks, and an avalanche thundered into a valley surrounded by white sprays of snow, as a distant and melancholy horn theme dissolved in Rudi's mind into a cataclysm of orchestral sounds and a hundred unmusical noises. The tank blurred; a wisp of smoke rose from a connection leading to it, and Jay leaped forward with an exclamation.

It was over.

Hoping that the breakdown had not outweighed the pleasure Rudi had shown, Howson turned to the bed. His hope was fulfilled. Rudi was struggling to sit up, his face radiant.

Howson cut across his incoherent babble of thanks with a calming thought. "You don't need to thank me," he said with a twisted smile. "I can tell you're pleased! You were stupid to think of giving up when success was in your grasp, weren't you?"

"But it wasn't!" Rudi protested. "If it hadn't been for you—and Clara, of course . . . But . . . but damnation, this isn't success, if I have to rely on you to help me."

"Rely on *me?*" Howson was genuinely astonished.

"Oh! I suppose you think I was projecting your imagery to Clara!" Succinctly he explained the actual situation. Relief grew plain on Rudi's face, but soon faded as he turned to Clara.

"Clara, how do you feel about this? You won't want to act as an interpreter for me indefinitely, for goodness' sake!"

"I'd like to do it for a while," she answered shyly. "But it won't always have to be done this way. Gerry says that the work we two can do together will excite people enough to show them what you're really after, and let you work with a full orchestra. And you can learn to use this thing yourself; Jay's made it so simple it only took me a few hours to get the hang of it. And eventually . . ."

She appealed wordlessly to Howson, who obliged by projecting the future he envisaged for Rudi's work directly into his mind.

There was a hall—vast, in darkness. At the far end lights glowed over music stands, and there was rustling and tuning up to be heard. Stillness was broken by the opening bars of Rudi's composition. Darkness was interrupted by the creation in a huge counterpart of Jay's yard-square tank of vivid, fluid, pictorial, corresponding images. The response in the audience could be felt, grew almost tangible, and in turn the brilliance of the imagery fed on the appreciation it evoked.

He finished, and found Rudi with his eyes closed and his hands clasped together on the coverlet. Howson got to his feet and beckoned his companions, and stealthily they crept from the room, leaving Rudi with the vision of his ambition fulfilled.

Later they sat in Jay and Charma's apartment celebrating their success with wine. "You—you didn't exaggerate at all, did you, Gerry?" Clara asked timidly when they had toasted him half a dozen times.

"Not much. Oh, slightly, perhaps; I mean, the sort of worldwide acclaim I promised him may take twenty years to come. But it damned well should come; Rudi has a gift as outstanding in its way as yours and mine. I'm sorry, you two," he added to Jay and Charma. "I didn't mean to sound conceited."

Jay shrugged. "I'll not deny I'd like to have some special talent, as you two have; but hell, it must entail a lot of heartbreak, too. I think I'll be a success in my own small way, and I doubt if I'll have the frustrations Rudi or yourselves will undergo."

"I'm glad you take it like that," Howson said thoughtfully. "And . . . you know, I've been giving the matter a little consideration, and I believe I could open up a market for as many of your fluid mobiles as you care to build. They have a certain restful fascination about them. . . . Suppose I recommended you to my director in chief and interested him in the idea of using them in place of the standard mobiles and tanks of tropical fish we use in the mental wards—especially for autistic children. You wouldn't think that was demeaning to your art, would you?"

"Good heavens, no!" said Jay, staring. "What do you think I make myself out to be—a second Michelangelo? I'm a glorified interior decorator, is all."

"And even if he did make himself out to be a genius," said Charma with mock grimness, "I'd cure him of the delusion quick enough. Thanks a million, Gerry; I'd practically given up hope of any return from these wet fireworks of his."

Then she looked directly at Howson.

"What about you? What have you got out of all this? It wouldn't be fair if there wasn't anything."

"Me?" Howson chuckled. "I've got just about everything. The mere fact that I've had it for years without realizing doesn't make me any less pleased. You see . . . Well, Rudi, so to speak, has just given his first public performance. I think I might go ahead and give mine."

He had been looking forward to this moment; indeed, he had had difficulty containing himself so long. He reached out gently with his mind and began to tell a story.

How could he have been so blind? How could he have failed to realize that the solution to his problem was here, under his nose?

He—Gerry Howson—had more power behind his telepathic voice than anyone had ever had, even Ilse Kronstadt. So why should he have to lock himself and his audience away into a catapathic grouping to prevent the outside world from breaking the flow of pleasurable fantasy? All he needed was a degree of concentration about as deep as people achieved of their own accord when they were carried away by brilliant acting or great music.

Moreover, he wasn't so disillusioned with reality that he needed to hide from it. What he craved wasn't the exercise of unbridled power, or any of the other unfeasible yearnings which a telepathist had to retreat into fugue to let loose. He wanted acceptance. He wanted to wipe out the legacy of twenty years during which he was *only* a runt with a bum leg, and people judged him entirely on that basis. Put at its simplest, he wanted to make friends with the world that had been hostile to him.

And he could.

He conjured up a simple fantasy, a fairy tale, with sights, sounds, smells, tactile sensations, emotions—all drawn from the vast store of unreal and real memory with which his intimate knowledge of so many minds beside his own had armed him. It was only a trial run, of course. One day there would be something more. But for now, this was enough.

His audience came slowly back to the present, eyes shining, and he knew he had won.

And now?

Maybe a trip around the world to add a knowledge of reality to his knowledge of other people's dreams and nightmares and imaginings, drawing here a litttle and there a little from the consciousness of Asians, Europeans, Americans, Australasians. . . . The whole world lay open to him now.

He smiled, and poured himself more wine.

As usual the stadium had been packed to capacity. The very rarity of the occasions on which Gerald Howson invited people to hear him "thinking aloud" ensured that all available accommodation went as soon as it was advertised; he never allowed this to conflict with his work at Ulan Bator therapy center. But whenever he got the opportunity, he would notify some city with a suitable arena or hall, and people would travel a thousand miles if they could manage it. In two years he had achieved a reputation on every continent.

Tonight he had coped with his biggest audience yet—almost five thousand. Now they were wistfully filing from the exits, and Howson was receiving—and largely ignoring—the inevitable wave of congratulations from distinguished listeners. As always, he had to keep denying that he was tired after his efforts; perhaps he should explain as a coda to the performance that he did this at least in part to refresh himself after a tough period of work. He never felt so relaxed and happy as after one of these rare public appearances.

Tonight he had skipped from idea to idea, now telling his audience of his work, now telling them the thoughts of a normal happy person, in India, in Venezuela, in Italy, in many other places where he had garnered his material. It had become a virtuoso achievement; often he improvised on the reactions of the members of the audience, leaving those who were lonely and unhappy proud to have been singled out. And always, if there was anyone present laboring under an intolerable problem, he found someone else, generally an influential official, and left the suggestion that something be done to right matters.

Ilse, Ilse! If you had stumbled on this you would not have died so burdened with regret!

"Gerry," said Pandit Singh softly through the babble of voices. "Gerry, there's someone here whom you ought to see."

Hullo, Rudi. I knew you were there. Just give me a chance to get rid of these so-and-so's!

A silent suggestion that the onlookers should take their leave, and he was free to come and shake Rudi's hand. Clara was with him, and he greeted her affectionately.

How are you?

Fine! You'll be seeing a lot of me from now on. I start training as a therapy watchdog at Ulan Bator next month.

Delight!

"Hullo, Gerry," said Rudi, unaware of this mental exchange. He seemed almost embarrassed. "You were wonderful."

"I know," said Howson, smiling. Rudi could hardly recognize him as the same person, so greatly had his new self-assurance transfigured him. "When are you going to join me in show business?"

"I'm giving my first performance in a few weeks. Mainly, I came to invite you and make sure you can be there. If you can't, I'll postpone it. I'm determined to have you in on the first night."

"Congratulations! You may be sure I'll come—emergencies permitting."

Rudi glanced sidelong at Pandit Singh. A slight flush colored his cheekbones. "Gerry . . . I've been talking with Dr. Singh here, about you, and I've been finding out quite a lot about your—uh—your disability. I don't know much about either medicine or telepathy, but I seem to have come up with an idea that's not as foolish as I thought it might be. Ah . . . as I understand it, the trouble is that some part of your brain which ought to look after the repair and upkeep of your body has been sacrificed to your telepathic organ."

"Roughly," confirmed Howson. He searched Rudi's face keenly, but the evident tension there held him back from forestalling his next words. In his own mind he felt a taut premonition.

"Well, what I was thinking was . . . if you can transfer practically anything from another person's mind to your own, couldn't you sort of borrow the necessary part of *my* mind to make up for what you haven't got?" The last part came in a rush, and Rudi looked at once hopeful and excited. "You see, I owe you everything, including my life, and I'd like to do something equally valuable in return."

The world was spinning around Howson. He stared at Pandit Singh, mutely inquiring whether this thing could be.

"I've hardly had a chance to think it through," Singh said. "But at first glance I don't see any reason why it shouldn't be tried. It might mean that your bodily appearance would tend toward Mr. Allef's, but it also holds out the hope of our being able to operate on you and give you a chance of healing normally. It might even mean your growing in height. I've warned Mr. Allef that it would mean lying in a hospital bed as long as was required, unable to do anything and enduring as much pain as if he himself had been operated on, and that with no sure promise of success—"

"And I still insist on being allowed to do it," said Rudi firmly.

Howson closed his eyes. He could do nothing else but accept, of course, but even as he uttered grateful words he felt it was unnecessary. Whether or not this hope were granted, whether or not the operation were successful, was of little account. For in the moment when Rudi made his offer, he, Gerald Howson, had become a whole man.

Lester del Rey

Available at your bookstore or use this coupon.

DEL REY

LARRY NIVEN
Science Fiction Superstar!

☐ A GIFT FROM EARTH	24509	1.50
☐ A HOLE IN SPACE	27137	1.50
☐ A WORLD OUT OF TIME	25750	1.75
☐ ALL THE MYRIAD WAYS	27133	1.50
☐ FLIGHT OF THE HORSE	25577	1.50
☐ FLYING SORCERERS, Larry Niven with David Gerrold	25307	1.75
☐ THE LONG ARM OF GIL HAMILTON	25808	1.50
☐ NEUTRON STAR	24794	1.50
☐ THE PROTECTOR	24778	1.50
☐ RINGWORLD	24795	1.50
☐ TALES OF KNOWN SPACE	24563	1.50
☐ WORLD OF PTAVVS	24591	1.50

 Ballantine Mail Sales
Dept. LE, 201 E. 50th Street
New York, New York 10022

Please send me the books I have checked above. I am enclosing
$........................ (please add 50¢ to cover postage and handling).
Send check or money order—no cash or C.O.D.'s please.

Name_____

Address_____

City_____State_____Zip_____

Please allow 4 weeks for delivery.

Available at your bookstore or use this coupon.